NO TI
BE ALONE

DANIEL HURST

www.danielhurstbooks.com

Download My Free Book

If you would like to receive a FREE copy of my psychological thriller 'Just One Second', then you can find the link to the book at my website www.danielhurstbooks.com

PROLOGUE

The snowflakes that began to fall on the morning of the 24th December gave almost everybody in this town hope that it might just be a white Christmas after all. Almost everybody because there were a few people who didn't want the roads and pavements to be covered in white powder, such as nervous drivers and those who found themselves a little unsteady on their feet at the best of times.

One of those people was making her way to the bus stop now, and as the flurry grew a little stronger, blowing wisps of white snow around her grey hair, the old lady in the blue coat clutching a bunch of flowers in her hand kept her head low and her steps short. She had to be careful not to slip on this icy pavement and not just because she didn't want to spend Christmas in hospital listening to some doctor tell her which bone she might have broken. It was because she had an important job to do today. It might have been the holiday season, but some people never took a day off from their duties, and the woman with the flowers in her hand was one of them.

Having made it to the bus stop without incident, the lady took refuge under the shelter and checked the thin watch on her wrist to see what time it was. Seeing that it was ten o'clock, she knew that the bus should be along here in a moment, and it couldn't come a minute too soon. It really was cold, and there were much better places for a woman in her seventies to be than standing on a frosty street waiting for a lift. But as the minutes ticked by, it became clear the bus was running late.

It had to be.

It had never been early in all the years she had lived here.

It was a little after ten when the elderly lady boarded the bus that would take her from the corner of her street all the way to the church across town. She secured her fare by taking out her bus pass after removing it from her handbag, the bag her husband, Bill, had bought for her seventieth birthday three years ago. She gave her pass to the driver, along with a warm greeting too, wishing him a good morning and not wasting her time grumbling about the fact that the bus was a couple of minutes late. She assumed it wasn't the driver's fault and was most likely down to the traffic around these parts. It had become heavier over the years as more houses had been built and more people had moved into the area. It was certainly very different now to how it had been when she had moved here fifty years ago with Bill, their first home together turning out to be their only home together. But neither of them had seen any reason to move. They had been happy where they lived and had many wonderful memories. A few new-builds and a little extra traffic wasn't going to spoil all of that.

After receiving her pass back from the driver, who surely hadn't needed to inspect it so thoroughly, the woman made her way tentatively down the aisle that ran through the centre of the bus, glad that she no longer had to negotiate the busy roads around here anymore. That was because she had given up driving last year on the advice of her doctor, who had told her that her eyesight was not up to what was required, even with the strong prescription glasses she wore. It seemed they just didn't make glasses with lenses strong enough for her to be road-worthy any longer.

Some people might have taken offence at being told they were better off the roads than on them, but this patient hadn't minded. She had simply smiled at her doctor, accepted his words, and then asked him how his daughter was doing, the one who was in university studying to become a vet. She always asked about the doctor's daughter because she had been going to the same surgery ever since moving to this area, and because of that, she had been seeing the same doctor for over half of that time. Doctor Terrence was his name. He was a lovely man, and he had a pretty photo of his daughter on his desk that he often updated over the years as she grew up. But on that last visit, Doctor Terrence had frowned a little when she had asked about his daughter at the end of their consultation and while he didn't say why, she had realised a moment later.

He was frowning because she had already asked him that day. She had asked him when she had first entered his office and taken her seat beside his desk. The fact she had asked again only a few minutes later, as if they hadn't already had that conversation, was evidence of another thing that was starting to fail in her body.

Her memory.

Just like her eyesight, it wasn't as sharp as it used to be. But it wasn't completely gone yet, far from it, and she was still capable of looking after herself, which was why the doctor hadn't been as concerned as he might otherwise have been. But time was ticking as it always did, and both the doctor and the patient knew that there would most likely come a day in the near future when they would have to have a more serious conversation about that brain of hers.

Reaching one of the empty seats on the bus, the weary passenger lowered herself carefully down into it while feeling grateful that the driver had waited patiently for her to sit before putting his vehicle back into motion again. He was a true gentleman, she thought, because some drivers would just put their foot down the second that she had passed them, and that had sometimes resulted in her having to desperately reach out for something to hold on to, or she would have toppled to the floor. But this driver was not like some of the others. He was respecting his elders and clearly had the awareness within him that it was only a matter of time until he was the old person on the bus shuffling his way to a seat.

That was something the youth of today never seemed to grasp as they ran around, pushing and shoving people with their headphones in and their mobile phones in their hands. They didn't seem to grasp that they would be old eventually too and when they were, they would very much appreciate it if the youngsters around them weren't so loud, reckless, and rude.

Speaking of the youth of today, the elderly passenger could hear some commotion coming from the back of the bus as it set off towards the next stop, and when she turned around, she saw that there were a couple of teenagers sitting on the back seat, listening to very loud music on their phone. They were two boys and looked to be around fourteen or fifteen, but they both caught the old woman looking at them before she had a chance to turn back around.

'What are you looking at, Grandma?' one of the boys asked her, his tone of voice letting everybody on this bus know just how he felt about a stranger making eye contact with him.

The woman who had been caught looking turned around in her seat and fixed her eyes on the front of the bus, not wishing to do anything that might aggravate the teenagers further because it was obvious that they were spoiling for an argument if they could get one. But despite that, the teens seemed intent on having their fun with her, and they proceeded to turn their music up even louder, to the point where it was almost deafening.

The elderly woman shook her head and looked around at the other passengers in the hope that one of them might be bold enough to ask the boys at the back if they could be a little quieter. But none of them seemed eager to volunteer to do such a thing, and those who hadn't already put their headphones in to drown out the noise just sat and stared out of the window as if their eardrums weren't being assaulted by the music from the back.

That was the problem these days. Everybody was too scared to speak up because no one knew what kind of reaction it would provoke. A person might be well within their rights to ask for the music to be turned down, but who knew how the teenagers would react? Would they hurl abuse? Throw fists? Or worst of all, pull out a knife?

It was those fears that were prompting everybody to keep to themselves, and it was the same reason why the elderly lady with the handbag on her lap ultimately kept quiet too.

She didn't want any trouble.

Not today, of all days.

The bus trundled on along its familiar route, stopping and starting again until twenty minutes had passed, and the old woman reached out to press the button that would let the driver know that she wished to get off at the next stop.

As the bus slowed down and she rose to her feet, she felt something hit the back of her head, and when she turned around to look at what it was, she saw a crumpled-up leaflet that had been fashioned into a ball, presumably so it had been easier to throw at its intended target.

There were no prizes for guessing where the object had come from, and the elderly passenger looked towards the two teens on the back seat. That was when she saw them both grinning at her as if they were proud of themselves for what they had just accomplished.

With the bus stationary and every other person on it being held up now until she disembarked, the old lady decided to just get off instead of asking the teenagers why they had thrown something at her. The sounds of their sniggering as she got off the bus and stepped down onto the wet concrete of the pavement were particularly irritating, but on the bright side, she no longer had to listen to their awful music.

As the bus drove away, the disembarked passenger noted that there were a lot more flakes of snow falling from the ghostly sky overhead, so she reached into her handbag to take out her umbrella. She carried it everywhere with her at this time of year because as far as British winter essentials go, an umbrella was up there with gloves and a thick coat. But it wasn't easy to get it out and get it extended while trying to keep hold of her bunch of flowers too, and it took her a little while to get herself sorted.

With the umbrella opened up and now keeping the snow off her grey hair, the old lady set off down the street in the direction of the large iron gates that stood in the gap between two tall, stone walls. This was a place she had been fortunate enough to not have to frequent for most of her life, but now it was starting to become familiar to her, a new part of her weekly routine that was certainly not as much fun as the other parts like Bingo and coffee with an old friend.

Passing through the iron gates that were always unlocked and open between the hours of 06:00-2100, the elderly visitor started along the path that cut through this cemetery, keeping her eyes on the ground before her rather than on the dreary sights that surrounded her. She chose to look at the concrete path rather than at the dozens of headstones that stuck out of the ground because there weren't many people who liked to be reminded of death, and this seventy-three-year-old was no different. There would come a time when she was laid to rest here, but it wouldn't be today. Unlike the rest of these poor souls, she still had some living to do yet.

It only took her four minutes from the gate to reach the gravestone she was here to visit, and when she did, she stopped and looked at the inscription upon it. It contained the words that she had chosen to be carved into this stone back when she had been making funeral arrangements, and they were the words that she felt best summed up how she felt about the man whose resting place this was.

Bill Wainwright 1947-2021
Beloved husband to Barbara.
Adored father to Tony.
Rest In Peace.

There were tears in the elderly woman's eyes as she looked down at her husband's headstone, but they weren't a result of emotion and were actually just down to the icy wind that was sweeping across this cemetery and blowing into her face. She was too old and too long in the tooth to find herself weeping for anything these days, so she just put her flowers down and said a silent hello to Bill before letting out a sigh and turning back to the gates.

She knew she wouldn't be the only one to visit this place today and pay their respects to a lost loved one. After all, a big part of living was remembering the dead. And Barbara would always remember. She remembered everything. Her doctor might disagree with that statement, but she knew she was a long way from losing her marbles yet.

She was alive, and as long as that was the case, she could still enjoy herself.

And what better time to enjoy herself than Christmas.

1

The white vistas that were whizzing past Nicola Peterson's train window really did look quite magical. So much so that she decided to take out her phone and see if she could capture a video of the snow-covered fields as she passed them by. But either the quality of her camera wasn't good enough or the vehicle she was travelling in was going too fast because all she ended up with was blurry footage that didn't at all capture the picturesque scene she had been hoping to record.

Rolling her eyes and putting the phone down on the small tray table in front of her, Nicola consoled herself about her poor video-making skills by taking another cookie out of the packet she had bought at the station just before her train had left London. It was a packet that had been very full when the train had rolled out of Euston, but now that she was in the Midlands, the contents had become somewhat sparser.

It would have been easy for her to feel a little guilty about the fact that she had consumed so many calories on her journey so far, but she reconciled those feelings by reminding herself that it was almost Christmas, and everybody overindulged at this time of year. Tomorrow was about turkey and all the trimmings, but today could just as easily be about eating too much and feeling sick for hours afterwards. Christmas Eve was practically Christmas Day, so Nicola wasn't going to worry about cleaning up her diet until the new year now.

Besides, she was technically on holiday at this moment in time, even if it didn't quite feel like a typical break.

The reason for this trip not feeling the same as a traditional holiday was because Nicola had travelled to England, and as this was the country she had been born and raised in, she could be forgiven for not feeling full of wonderous excitement about being back here. There would be no exotic beaches or cold cocktails beside a pool on this trip, so did that even make it a holiday? Nicola wasn't sure. All she knew was that she was back in her native land, and very soon she would be home properly, sitting on the sofa at her parents' house and being bombarded with all the memories of her childhood.

Think less of a sandy beach and more of a photo album full of embarrassing pictures.

It wasn't that Nicola was disappointed to be back in England because she was definitely not. This was a much-needed chance to catch up with family and friends again, all the people she had missed so much while she had been living her new life on the other side of the world.

It had been three years ago when Nicola had first departed the English shores to start a new life in Australia, her mind and body eager for a change of scene and a challenge. Packing up and moving abroad alone would be a big change for anybody to undertake, but it had been especially difficult for Nicola because she had been thirty-five at the time she had taken the leap. At that age, most people had already gotten all their crazy dreams and wishes out of their system and settled down, starting families and securing their step somewhere on a career ladder. But Nicola had defied convention and decided that she wanted to make a fresh start in her life at a time when all her friends were having babies, paying bills, and saving the remains in that open bottle of wine in the fridge for another day.

Her decision to leave her home country and start afresh in the land Down Under had taken all her friends by surprise, but that was nothing compared to the shock that her parents had displayed when she had informed them of her decision. Nicola's father, John, had been dumbfounded by the news that she had not only applied for a nurse's job in Sydney but had been accepted, while her mother, Ruth, had just gone very quiet and looked like she had tears in her eyes.

Nicola's plan for the next chapter of her life had never been created with the intention of upsetting her parents, but she had been forced to admit that was a price she had to pay if she was going to go through with her decision. She had come to realise that moving to Australia was the best thing for her personally, but with that came sacrifice, and it came in the form of having to say a teary goodbye to all of her loved ones. Along with her parents, who had tried and ultimately failed to talk her out of what she was planning, Nicola had said an emotional goodbye to her brother, Colin, her sister-in-law, Charlotte, and her three-year-old nephew, Ben, at the airport on the day she had boarded her flight from Manchester to Sydney, via a short stopover in Singapore. The little boy had been the hardest one to say farewell to because unlike the adults he had been with, he hadn't really been able to grasp the enormity of what was happening. Nicola's other relatives had known that they wouldn't be seeing her for a very long time as they had hugged and kissed at the departure gate, but Ben had no idea that his auntie was going to be disappearing out of his life for the majority of the time now. That had been why Nicola had found herself wiping away tears as she had hugged the little boy before forcing herself to pick up her suitcase and pass through the gate before she had any time for more doubts to creep in and stop her from boarding that plane.

Having spent the first hour of the flight staring blankly at the back of the seat in front of her and wondering if she had made a mistake, Nicola had managed to snap out of her trance and remind herself that she was doing the right thing in her life. She was getting away from her past and hurtling headlong through the sky at hundreds of miles an hour towards a brighter future.

And so it had proved.

Well, for the most part, anyway.

Nicola had stepped off the plane in Sydney, exhausted and aching but with a spring in her step as she had passed all the tourism signs at the airport that reminded her that she really was in a very different place now. Images of the iconic Opera House and Harbour Bridge had greeted her as she had wheeled her suitcase towards the passport control desks, and once through those checks, she had seen a man with a didgeridoo performing for all the excited tourists who had just landed on these unfamiliar shores. Nicola had been sure to record a video of the performance to send back to her loved ones before she had climbed into the back of a taxi and instructed the driver to take her to her first port of call in this new country. It had been a hotel overlooking Circular Quay, the busy harbour area home to many of Sydney's most famous landmarks and the place where Nicola could rest her weary head and sleep off the jet lag that came with flying to the other side of the world in twenty-four hours.

But it had proven difficult to sleep that first night in Australia and not just because she was missing her loved ones back home and experiencing that sinking feeling in her stomach that often accompanied a traveller who was in an unfamiliar place. It was because she had never been a good sleeper, certainly not in adulthood anyway, and while what she had wasn't quite as bad as insomnia, sometimes it felt worse than that.

The thing was that Nicola could drift off to sleep.

She just usually woke up screaming a few hours later.

The root cause of her nightmares was one she had done her best to bury down deep inside herself over the years, preferring not to look back and dwell on the past because she knew as well as anybody that the past couldn't be changed. That was why she always tried so hard to focus on what was ahead of her instead, and the decision to move to Australia had been a part of that life-plan to prioritise the future over what had gone before. But as most people who were running from their past would know, that was easier said than done, and despite being over 16,000 miles from the source of her pain, Nicola had still felt just as fearful as before.

A sudden shake of the train carriage snapped the passenger out of her daydream, and Nicola looked away from the window and back at the packet of cookies in front of her. There was only one left now, and that meant she must have eaten one while she was in her trance, which was unfortunate because she hadn't been concentrating enough on it to really get the full benefit of all those extra calories. But as she contemplated whether or not to finish off the last biscuit and dispose of the packet so that there was no evidence of what she had just done, she heard a male voice speak to her from across the carriage.

'Go on. Have the last one. It's Christmas.'

Nicola looked up to see who had just spoken to her, and when she saw who it was, she felt even more ashamed of herself for gorging on calorific snacks. That's because it was a handsome passenger who Nicola would certainly have made more of an effort to look better in front of if she had noticed him sitting across the aisle from her.

'Thanks for trying to make me feel better, but I think I've eaten enough,' Nicola replied with a smile before she picked up the tray with the last cookie in it and held it out towards the good-looking guy. He looked like he spent more time in the gym than in the confectionery aisle of his local supermarket, but she felt it was worth a try.

'I shouldn't,' the man replied as he eyed the cookie hungrily. 'But if you're sure?'

'I insist,' Nicola replied, and the man laughed before reaching out and gratefully accepting the cookie.

Watching the man eating the same unhealthy food she had just been eating made Nicola feel a little better about her diet choices on this train journey, but as she checked the time on her phone, she saw that there was still an hour of this journey to go. She was due into Manchester Piccadilly at 10:55, but there was still some time to kill before then, and with that in mind, Nicola thought about taking her headphones from her handbag and listening to a little music. That was until the handsome stranger spoke again.

'So, are you heading home for the holidays too?' he asked her after finishing the cookie and washing it down with a swig from his bottle of water.

'Yeah, I'm going back to my parents,' Nicola replied. 'You?'

'Same. There were some big parties being planned in London, but I thought I should be a good son and show my face at Christmas dinner this year.'

Nicola smiled, and she knew how this man felt because she had also had the option of doing a few things that sounded a little more exciting than going home for Christmas, namely parties on Bondi Beach and sunbathing instead of shivering under three layers of clothing. It was summertime in Australia right now, but she had swapped it for ten days back in the freezing cold of a British winter, although it was best not to dwell on that, or she might feel like getting off this train and heading to the nearest airport.

'Now, either there is a very tropical part of London that I am missing out on, or you must have got that tan somewhere else,' the man said a moment later, clearly having noticed how sun-kissed Nicola's skin was. 'Have you been away?'

'Yeah, kind of,' she replied. 'I live in Australia.'

'Wow, really? That's amazing.'

'It's okay. The pubs aren't as good as they are over here, and I never know if the spider on my bedroom wall is capable of killing me with one bite, but apart from that, it's great.'

The man laughed, and while that should have made Nicola feel good, seeing a member of the opposite sex seemingly enjoy her company so much only reminded her of the fact that she very rarely chatted with guys, never mind flirted with them.

'Fair enough. I guess it has its pros and cons just like anywhere else,' the man replied. 'But where's the hunky Australian you've brought back to introduce to your parents? I can't see any tanned and toned guys on this train with a surfboard under their arm.'

The man pretended to look around the carriage for Nicola's 'Aussie boyfriend', but she just laughed and told him that she was travelling alone. But perhaps that had been what the man had been seeking to clarify all along because no sooner had she confirmed that she was single then he introduced himself formally.

'I'm Jack,' he said with a smile before offering his hand across the aisle for Nicola to shake.

But she paused before taking it, as well as hesitating before giving her own name, and while it was only a slight delay, it was long enough for Jack to get the impression that his pick-up attempt might not have been going as well as he had thought.

'I'm sorry,' he said, moving his hand away rather sheepishly after it had failed to be grasped by the woman across the aisle from him. 'I was just trying to be friendly.'

'No, it's fine,' Nicola said, suddenly realising how rude she must have appeared. 'I'm sorry, I'm just a little tired from the flight over from Oz.'

'I understand,' Jack replied, and he smiled again, although the expression didn't have quite as much warmth in it as it had done the first few times Nicola had seen it. Then he picked up his phone and started texting on it, and the woman he had just been talking to realised she had just messed up this exchange with her nervousness.

Cursing the fact that she had once again proven to be useless with the opposite sex, Nicola turned and looked out of her window again at the fields that were continuing to be doused in a hearty helping of snow. She lamented the fact that she had always been this way with men, and it was the reason why she was approaching forty and had yet to ever have a serious relationship. But her story wasn't one of cheating partners and a string of bad luck. She had just stayed single all these years because she found it difficult to be intimate with anybody after what she had been through.

Because of her past experiences and her wish to avoid any situation that might stir up more of those terrible memories, Nicola resorted to mostly keeping herself to herself, only ever talking to men if they spoke to her first. As an attractive woman, it was quite common for a guy to strike up a conversation with her, but even then, Nicola had her tricks to avoid things progressing too far. Like lying, for example. She had just told Jack that she was tired from her flight over from Australia, but that was not true. The truth was that she had actually landed in London three days ago, and having recovered from her jet lag, she had spent the time since then catching up with friends in the capital and having fun in good old British pubs before boarding this train that was taking her north. But she had opted for a white lie rather than the truth, and coupled with her reluctance to shake Jack's hand, Nicola was once again left alone and faced spending the rest of this journey in silence.

Looking across the aisle at the man who had been nothing but polite and witty with her, she felt bad for not making more of an effort to keep their exchange going. But despite that, she also felt like she had done the right thing. After all, what would be the point of carrying on the conversation and giving this guy the impression that it could lead somewhere? Presumably, he would have asked for her number and hinted at grabbing a drink together some time over the holidays if they had kept chatting all the way to Manchester, and while that would have been lovely, Nicola would have ultimately had to disappoint him, if not today, then after their date. She would have disappointed him by shying away when it came to the moment when he might have moved in for a kiss, or considering how little time they would have had before she left the country again, invited her to go somewhere more private. Therefore, it had been best to just nip this thing in the bud now before it became anything bigger.

It was just a friendly chat between strangers on a train.

And it was just another example of why Nicola was heading home to see her family after three years away without a man by her side to introduce to them.

2

Having spent most of her life in the North of England, Nicola would have thought she would have been better accustomed to the drop in temperatures, even after spending the last three years in warmer climes. But it seemed her time away from home had reduced her body's ability to handle the cold weather, and as she stood outside the train station and looked for her dad, she felt as if she could freeze solid in the midst of this snowstorm.

Where was he? He was supposed to be collecting his daughter and driving her home so that she didn't have to get another train and extend her long journey by another forty minutes. But Nicola couldn't see him anywhere in this car park full of other people being collected by their loved ones, and the longer she stood there, the more she felt like she was losing all feeling in her face and hands.

'The wanderer returns!'

Nicola heard the familiar voice over her shoulder and turned around to see her dad, John, standing before her, his arms wide open and his face displaying just how happy he was to see her after all this time.

'Come here!' he said before enveloping his offspring in a tight bear hug that she barely had a chance to prepare for. But Nicola didn't mind because she had missed this man just as much as he had clearly missed her, and it felt good for her to be wrapped in his arms again, almost as good as it felt when she was a child and relied on his protection.

'Look at the colour of you! I thought you were working over there, not sunbathing all day!' John cried, displaying his trademark sarcastic humour before relieving Nicola of her heavy suitcase and pointing out where he had parked.

'We're over there,' he told her, gesturing across the car park. 'Sorry I'm late. The traffic was a nightmare. The roads are full of snow and last minute Christmas shoppers.'

Nicola smiled as she joined her father in walking across the slush-covered car park, and he asked about her train journey as they went. She filled him in on some of the details but chose to leave out a couple of parts, namely all the cookies she had eaten on the way and the ultimately disappointing exchange with the handsome stranger across the aisle from her.

'I hope you're hungry,' John said as they reached the car. 'You should see all the food your mother has bought. The fridge is literally groaning under the weight of it all.'

Nicola laughed as she opened the passenger door and slid into the seat, relieved to be out of the snow now and inside the car, although it wasn't much warmer in here.

'Which one turns the heater on?' Nicola asked as she started pressing some of the buttons that were connected to the dashboard of her father's car. But he was able to stop her before she pressed anything that could cause too much havoc before flicking the correct switch, and it was only a moment later when hot air began to blow out of the vents and warm up the car's two occupants.

No longer fearing death by cold weather, Nicola relaxed into her seat as her dad put the car into motion and steered them through the busy car park towards the exit. The outside of the car was full of train passengers hugging loved ones, and it was clear that plenty of people had made the journey here today to be home for Christmas, just like Nicola had. She smiled as she saw some of the interactions passing by her window, including one of a young boy wrapping his arms tightly around the legs of who she presumed was the child's grandmother, and it warmed her heart almost as much as the heaters were warming the rest of her.

But then Nicola saw something that made her feel a little uncomfortable. It was Jack, the guy she had spoken to on the train, and he was walking right in front of the car.

'He needs to look where he's going,' John moaned as he was forced to hit the brake pedal and bring his vehicle to a stop so as not to hit the man crossing in front of him.

Jack looked up through the windscreen of the car as he passed, and he made eye contact with Nicola, but she quickly averted her gaze, feeling shy about seeing the man one last time. Then he was gone, walking on, presumably in search of his own family to take him home, and she knew she would never see him again.

Like all the other men in her life, it had ended up being a complete non-event.

‘So, how does it feel to be back?’ John asked her as they travelled down the snow-covered streets with the man at the wheel forced into using the accelerator pedal a lot less than he would like due to these treacherous driving conditions.

‘It’s a bit weird,’ she replied.

‘I bet. I’m sure it’s not snowing in Australia right now.’

‘Nope, it was thirty-one degrees on the day I left.’

‘Wow, thirty-one degrees in December! That’s decided it then. Me and your mum are coming to stay with you next Christmas.’

Nicola smiled at her father inviting himself and her mother over to stay with her in Sydney, but she didn’t mind because, of course, they were always more than welcome to stay with her at the two-bedroom flat she had bought herself in the fashionable Eastern suburbs. It was the flat she had purchased after saving up enough in her new role as a nurse at one of the hospitals in the city, and alongside an improvement in the weather, Nicola had also noticed a big improvement in her finances since making the change. She had found that doing the same role in Australia as she had done in England paid her more money and came with a little less hassle, so she certainly didn’t regret changing work environments so dramatically. Nor did she regret buying her own place rather than renting with other people because she had managed to make enough friends amongst the other nurses at the hospital to ensure that her social life was healthy enough in her new country.

'I still talk about the last time we came to see you all the time, you know?' John said as they drove on through a set of green traffic lights. 'It was such a good holiday.'

'Yeah, it was,' Nicola confirmed, and her mind drifted back to that fortnight eighteen months ago when her parents had flown out to visit her.

John and Ruth had landed in Sydney and spent three days exploring the city that their daughter now called home, before the three of them had embarked on an adventure into the Outback, visiting Alice Springs and taking in the spectacular sight of Uluru at sunrise. Seeing that recognisable red rock with the first light of a new day spreading across it had truly been a breath-taking experience, and Nicola had been thrilled that she had got to have it with her loved ones. She had also been upset when she had needed to bid them both a farewell at the airport at the end of their stay, wishing them a safe flight and promising them that she would come for Christmas the year after that. Now she was here and had been good to her word, but this was a long way from those sizzling days in the Australian desert.

The snow was getting heavier as the clock counted down to Christmas Day.

The father-daughter duo chatted as they continued to drive across town, and while it was taking a lot longer than usual to make this journey, Nicola was happy enough with having this alone time with her father. That was because she knew that it would be very different when she got home and saw the rest of her family. John had told her that they were all waiting for her arrival, excited and eager to see her after so long and desperate to hear about what she had been up to on the other side of the world. Nicola wondered what new stories she might be able to tell them because she had already passed on most of them during the numerous video calls they had held while she had been away.

It had been important for Nicola to maintain a strong connection with her family, even though they were so many miles apart, because she knew how much they all missed her and feared never hearing from her again because there were surely more fun things for her to be doing than sitting in her flat talking to a computer screen. But she was always happy to schedule a call, and that was why she felt like she had already told her loved ones everything she had done since she had been working Down Under.

'What happened to the charity shop?' Nicola asked as the car passed by a once-familiar storefront around ten minutes from the family home.

'Oh, that went last year,' John replied matter-of-factly. 'It's an estate agency now.'

'No way, I loved that place,' Nicola cried, lamenting the fact that one of the few shops in her hometown that she actually liked shopping at had closed down. But it was just a reminder of how long she had been away from here and how nothing ever stayed the same.

'And the chip shop on the corner of Smith Street has gone,' John said as he turned a corner and took them onto another road. 'It's a pizza place now.'

'What? I loved the chips from there!'

‘You and me both, kid. But the pizzas aren’t that bad. We’ll have to get one while you’re back.’

Nicola liked the sound of having pizza one night while she was home, even if she didn’t like the sound of her favourite chip shop joining her favourite clothes shop in being consigned to this town’s history books.

‘What else has changed around here?’ she asked tentatively as John steered them onto their housing estate.

‘Not much apart from that,’ he replied, much to her relief. ‘None of the pubs have shut down yet, which is nothing short of a miracle the way the government have been putting taxes up for landlords over these last few years.’

Nicola smiled because she knew that as long as there were plenty of pubs in this town, then her father would be happy. She was also smiling because it meant there were still plenty of places that she could go for a drink with some of her old school friends while she was back, and she planned to see as many of them as she could once Christmas was out of the way. But for the next couple of days, Nicola’s world was going to revolve around spending quality time with her family, and as her dad turned the wheel of the car and took them onto the long road that led up to their house, she knew she was only a minute or so from home now.

She had spent many a night in Sydney wondering what it would feel like to back here again, but as the car moved up the street, passing some of their neighbours’ houses, Nicola realised she was experiencing a wide range of emotions. She was excited to see her other family members, of course, and she couldn't wait to sprawl out on the sofa in front of the TV and watch a Christmas movie while sipping on a glass of her father's homemade mulled wine. But she was also nervous too. She was nervous because this wasn't just a place where she felt safe like most people did when they returned to where they grew up.

This was also a place where she had been made to feel weak, insecure, and afraid.

Looking straight ahead through the windscreen, Nicola saw her family home come into view at the top of the street, and when she did, she couldn't help but laugh.

'Wow, somebody really went all out on the Christmas decorations this year,' she commented, and her father chuckled beside her.

'Guilty as charged. But I have to try and compete with the Morgans, don't I?' John replied, and he gestured towards one of the houses they were passing. It was a house that seemed to be almost covered from top to bottom in flashing lights, and even though it was still technically daylight, the gloomy weather ensured that the full effect of the extensive lighting was being seen by anybody who passed this property.

'Oh my God! Imagine how expensive their electricity bill must be to power all of that!' Nicola cried as she gawked at the garish house only a few doors down from her family home. But it was definitely the Morgan's place because she remembered them always overdoing it at this time of year, as if they were trying to win some kind of competition, even though most of the other neighbours didn't bother putting out so much as a *'Santa Stop Here'* sign.

'Yeah, I have no idea where they get half of that stuff from,' John muttered. 'But they seem to have more of it by the year. I think it must be their way of coping now Eric has finally moved out.'

Nicola knew who her father was talking about because she was the same age as Eric, and therefore, had grown up with him. The pair of them used to join some of the other kids in the neighbourhood and ride their bikes up and down this street, as well as playing hide and seek in the winter months when the darker nights made for a more interesting game. But Nicola had lost touch with Eric many years ago, around the time she had gone off to university and well before she even made the move over to Australia. But she had heard from her parents that Eric had been living at home all that time, and by all accounts, he had grown up to be a bit of a strange man. He was a 'wierdo' as Nicola's brother, Colin, would put it, but she didn't think of him as that.

Nicola knew he was just somebody who had been through a lot.

Just like she had.

But it had always been a shame that Eric had reacted much differently to the events of the past than Nicola had, and whilst she had opted to put her troubles behind her by spreading her wings and venturing out into the world, it had seemed like Eric had done the opposite, choosing to remain at home even when he was well into his thirties.

'He's moved out?' Nicola asked.

'Yeah, he's finally grown up and got his own place. A house on Chapel Street, I think his dad said. He's living by himself by all accounts, and I'm a little surprised he can afford it because he's still a janitor at the prison. I suspect his parents have helped him out with a little money, but at least he's not under their feet anymore.'

'Dad, that's not nice.'

'I'm sorry. But you know what I mean. Me and your mother love you to death, and you know we wish you were closer to home, but there's a big difference between living near home and never leaving it. It was about time Eric stood on his own two feet.'

Nicola decided not to say anything more on the matter because there wasn't much that she could add without making it obvious that she knew exactly why Eric had endured a very different life to most people his age. That was why she just turned away from the Morgan's house and looked back towards the house they were getting very near to now. But when she did, she saw somebody walking along the pavement in the same direction they were travelling in. It was an old lady in a blue coat, and she was clutching the straps of a handbag in one hand while holding the handle of an umbrella with the other.

'Is that Barbara?' John asked before Nicola could say anything. 'What the hell is she doing out here in this weather?'

Nicola knew it was their next-door neighbour, and while she had no idea why a woman of her age was out walking in the hazardous snow, she did know one thing.

It was a shock to see her again after all these years.

It was then that Nicola felt the car slowing down, and when she glanced across at the dashboard behind the steering wheel, she got confirmation that the speedometer was dropping.

'What are you doing?' Nicola asked her dad as the car continued to slow.

'I'm seeing if she's alright,' John replied before pressing the button that allowed the window on Nicola's door to electronically slide down.

'Why? Just keep going!' Nicola tried, but her dad had made his mind up, and he was stopping to check if their elderly neighbour needed help making it the rest of the way up this icy street.

'Hey, Barbara! You picked the wrong day for a walk,' John said, leaning over Nicola in the passenger seat and shouting out to the woman outside the car.

Barbara seemed surprised by the sudden sound of John's voice, and she almost dropped her umbrella before turning to look at the car. When she did, she got another surprise too.

'Oh my goodness, is that Nicola?' the old lady asked, peering at the woman in the passenger seat.

'Yeah, she's back from Australia for Christmas. Remember I mentioned it to you?' John replied, but Barbara shook her head as if it had slipped her mind before she took a small step closer to the open window to get a better look at the topic of conversation.

‘Oh my, look at you,’ Barbara said as she observed Nicola. ‘Somebody’s caught the sun.’

Nicola didn’t say a word to that, nor did she smile or do anything that might suggest she was prepared to engage in conversation. Instead, she just sat and stared straight ahead through the windscreen, wishing that her dad would just drive on so they could get inside their house.

‘Do you need a lift the rest of the way?’ John asked, gesturing to the backseat where he was making it obvious that Barbara was more than welcome to get in.

‘Oh, no. Don’t be silly. I’m almost home now. And I could do with the exercise.’

‘Are you sure? It’s slippery out here.’

‘Yes, I’m sure. I might be getting old, but I can still walk up my own street.’

John laughed at his elderly neighbour’s sharp reply before shrugging his shoulders and putting the car back into gear.

‘Okay then, well you be careful,’ he said before preparing to drive on, but just before he could, Barbara took one more step towards the vehicle and looked at Nicola again.

‘Welcome home,’ she said to the still-mute woman in the passenger seat, and while Nicola didn’t want to acknowledge that remark, she felt she had to when she noticed her dad was looking at her and waiting for her response.

‘Thanks,’ Nicola muttered before smiling weakly, but she didn’t look Barbara in the eyes as she spoke, and it was a relief when John put the car back into motion and allowed the window to go back up, shutting out the cold air as well as the old woman they had just been talking to.

'She's a hearty soul, isn't she?' John said as he drove onto the driveway of his house and finally brought the journey to an end.

But Nicola didn't answer that. Instead, she just kept her eyes on the wing mirror outside her car window that gave her a view of the street behind them.

She kept her eyes on the shape of the old lady shuffling her way through the snow.

3

'Is it me, or have you shrunk?'

Nicola rolled her eyes at her brother's inane question and made it clear that while she knew he had a duty as her big brother to wind her up, she also had a duty not to play into his hands.

'I think you're the one who has shrunk, bro,' Nicola replied as she patted him on the head. 'And it looks like you've lost a little hair too. Is that a bald spot?'

Colin suddenly looked concerned and put his hand to the top of his head, feeling the crown for any sign of a concerning bare patch in his hair follicles. But Nicola was only teasing him too, and he looked relieved when he realised that he wasn't actually losing his hair at all, although considering that he was forty and had a father who was decidedly thin on top, it seemed it was only a matter of time until poor Colin didn't need to go to the barbers as much anymore. And Nicola was only too happy to remind him of that fact.

'Play nice, you two,' their mother advised them as if they were still little children and not the grown adults they were supposed to be. But that was their mother all over. Ruth loved having her children at home, and even though it had been many years since they had been small and completely dependent on her, she still enjoyed looking after them, and she never missed a chance to tell them to stop being silly.

Nicola and Colin called a halt to their tormenting of each other, for now anyway, and went back to what they had been doing before, which was waiting for their dad to open the bottle of champagne so they could have a drink.

As John wrestled with getting the cork out of the bottle, Nicola knelt down and checked to see what her nephew, Ben, was up to because he was currently sitting on the floor of the kitchen and building some kind of structure with Lego.

'What's this going to be?' Nicola asked her nephew as she observed him deep in concentration while trying to put the finishing touches on what looked like a wall.

'It's my house,' Ben replied as if it was obvious what he was building. 'See, there's my room.'

He pointed to a section of the 'house', and Nicola did indeed see a bedroom, or what was supposed to be one anyway. It wasn't the best use of building blocks she had ever seen, but seeing as her nephew was only six, she knew that she should only encourage him, so she nodded her head and told him that it looked great.

As the cork was finally popped on the champagne bottle and the drinks started to be poured, Nicola spent a few more minutes on the floor with Ben, handing him pieces that he might find useful in his construction project while just enjoying the fact that she was getting to spend some time with him again. Three years was a long time to be away from home for anybody, but having now caught up with her parents, her brother, and her-sister-in law, Charlotte, as well as her friends down in London, Nicola had realised that they hadn't really changed much. But the same could not be said for her little nephew. He had grown so much since she had last seen him in person, and it was a reminder to her that there were sacrifices that had to be made for a life in the sun.

'What are we toasting to?' Colin asked as John handed out the champagne flutes that were now filled with fizzy liquid.

'What do you think we're toasting to?' Ruth replied. 'Your sister being home for Christmas, of course.'

'Oh, is that it?' Colin scoffed, but Nicola gave him a playful dig in the ribs, and he laughed before she received her champagne and prepared to take a sip.

But before she could drink, her dad had a few words to say.

'The whole family back together again under one roof,' John said with a satisfied smile as he looked around the ring of people standing before him in his kitchen while Ben continued to play by their feet.

'It really is nice to have you home for Christmas, Nicola. Thank you for making the long trip over to be with us. You know me and your mother are thrilled to have you back for the holidays, and he might not admit it, but I know your brother is too.'

Colin groaned, but Nicola enjoyed teasing her sibling a little more.

'I know this time is going to fly by as it tends to do, but I just want to say before all the craziness of Christmas kicks off in this house that I honestly feel like the luckiest man in the world to have a family like this one,' John added, making a few of the women in the room a little misty-eyed while Colin groaned again, and Ben continued to make a mess on the floor.

'Aww, that's lovely,' Charlotte said, and the rest of the women agreed. But her partner had heard enough.

'Are we drinking this champagne or not?' Colin asked before holding out his glass.

'Cheers,' John said as he clinked his glass against it.

'To the best Christmas ever,' Ruth chipped in before doing the same.

'It's good to be home,' Nicola added, and that was the last thing that was said before everybody put their glasses to their lips and drank.

Ten minutes later and the entire family was gathered in the much cosier setting of the living room, a Christmas movie on the television keeping young Ben entertained while the adults enjoyed their drinks and helped themselves to the many boxes of chocolates that had already been opened.

'I need to go on a serious diet when Christmas is over,' Charlotte commented. 'I swear I've already put on half a stone this month, and I've not even had Christmas dinner yet.'

'You and me both,' Ruth replied before shoving another chocolate into her mouth.

'What's it like over in Oz?' Charlotte asked Nicola from the opposing sofa. 'Do you feel under pressure to keep a bikini body because you all go to the beach so much?'

'My sister doesn't have a bikini body,' Colin interjected, but Nicola just threw one of her sweet wrappers at him before answering the question.

'Well, I'm not going to lie. It takes a lot of work to maintain a figure like this one,' she told her sister-in-law before reaching for the nearest chocolate tin and scooping out a handful of sugary treats.

Charlotte laughed, and Nicola experienced another moment of remembering something else she was missing by living on the other side of the world. She was missing having more girly chats with Charlotte, and that was a shame because the pair had always got on well, ever since Colin had first introduced his family to the new woman in his life. That had been a decade ago, and while the other family members had initially been a little sceptical about how long this latest romance would last, Colin had surprised them all by proposing to Charlotte only a year later, and then it was clear that she was the woman to tame his once wild ways.

That had been more than good news for Nicola, John, and Ruth, who had all been thrilled to welcome Charlotte into the family, and the wedding day that had come eight months later had been a wonderful occasion. But it had been nothing compared to the joy the family had felt when the happy couple had announced that they were expecting their first child, and the day that baby Ben was born was a day that none of them would ever forget.

Nicola had been preparing for another night shift at the town's hospital when she had got the call that the baby had arrived, and she had raced to the scene of the birth, fortunate that her place of work was also the place where Ben had been born, so she had been able to fit in a quick visit before starting her duties on another ward. It had been quite the moment when she had first held her nephew in her arms and not just because she had been beaming with pride at the life her big brother and his wife had created. It had also been because it was just another reminder that Nicola would never get to experience such a joyous moment as this as a mother herself.

It wasn't that she was physically unable to bear children. Rather, it was because she felt mentally unable to ever be able to not only start a serious relationship with a man, but sustain it too. It wasn't that she had never tried. It was just that it had never worked. Nicola was simply carrying too much baggage, and while she had never confided in anybody what that baggage entailed, she had kept any potential lovers at arm's reach, and that was why it was her brother sitting over there on that sofa with his wife beside him and his son playing on the floor, while she was sat on this sofa next to her mum with only a load of chocolates for company.

'This is a great Christmas film, isn't it?' John said from his armchair in between the two sofas, and everybody agreed that it was. All of them must have seen it a dozen times or more over the years because it was just one of many festive movies that got shown at this time of year, but they were all seemingly more than happy to sit through it again, and it was likely a scene that was being replicated all over the country right now.

It was Christmas Eve, and there was surely no better way to spend it.

But despite the happy setting and the presence of her loved ones, Nicola still felt uneasy. It was a feeling of unease that she had carried with her all day, ever since boarding the train at Euston, and it had only grown larger the closer that train had got to its destination. But it had really gone up a notch when she had seen Barbara out on the street on the way home.

Just like her family, it had been years since Nicola had seen her elderly neighbour.

But unlike her family, it was one person she had most definitely not missed.

Try as she might, Nicola found it increasingly difficult to concentrate on the light-hearted film on TV and instead, discovered that her mind kept drifting to the old woman next door. She wondered what she was doing now. Probably watching TV herself, or maybe reading a book. Bill would be somewhere nearby, no doubt, her husband by her side as he had always been. Those two were inseparable.

'Do you see much of Bill these days?' Nicola asked her parents after her curiosity got the better of her, and she decided to find out how he was doing. She had already seen Barbara today, of course, so there was no mystery there. But she was curious as to how her elderly husband was getting along.

But no sooner had she asked then she noticed her parents glance awkwardly at each other before delivering more news that Nicola had missed out on while she had been away.

'Oh, love. I'm sorry. I don't think we told you,' Ruth said, turning the volume down a little on the TV as she spoke. 'Bill passed away earlier this year.'

'What?'

It was a shock to Nicola, just like the news of anybody's death tended to be, but this was particularly surprising because the last she had known, he had been fit and well despite his advancing years.

'Yeah. It was a heart attack,' John solemnly informed his daughter. 'He'd had one just before that which had left him ill. Such a shame because he'd been fit as a fiddle before that first attack.'

'When?' Nicola wanted to know.

'I think it was February, wasn't it?' her mother replied.

'Yeah, that sounds about right,' John replied.

'Why didn't you tell me?'

'Well, we didn't want to upset you. And you were having a great time in Australia. We just figured we'd let you know the next time you were home.'

Nicola understood why her parents had kept this news from her, but it wouldn't have made a difference when they had given her it because it would have been a momentous occasion at any time. Looking back towards the TV with a dazed expression on her face, Nicola just stared at the moving images so that it appeared as if she was just watching the film with everybody else, but in reality, she wasn't really processing it, nor was she able to hear the words being spoken on screen.

She was stunned.

Bill was dead.

The rest of her family must have picked up on how upset she was because there was suddenly a little awkwardness in the room, and it was Charlotte who decided to be the one to broach the subject.

‘Were you close to Bill?’ she asked her sister-in-law, but Nicola didn’t answer the question, instead just continuing to stare at the TV and finding it increasingly more difficult to concentrate on anything. In the end, it was Ruth who answered that question on her daughter’s behalf.

‘Bill and Barbara used to babysit Nicola,’ she said. ‘We’d drop her off next door when we were taking Colin to his swimming competitions.

‘Awww, that’s cute,’ Charlotte replied, but Nicola barely heard that summation of her time spent with her neighbours.

‘Yeah, they were really helpful,’ Ruth went on. ‘Nicola hated going watching her brother swim. She found it really boring. But Bill and Barbara offered to watch her for us, and we took them up on it. It was a big help, wasn’t it?

‘Yeah, much easier than having her complaining all the way through Colin’s races,’ John mused as he recalled those past times when his children had been much younger.

‘Did they ever babysit for you?’ Charlotte asked her partner, but Colin just shrugged and made it clear he was more interested in watching the film than chatting about who took charge of his babysitting duties when he was a kid.

‘No, it was just Nicola, I think,’ Ruth answered for him. ‘She would have been around five or six. And she didn’t have as many activities as Colin back then. It took her a while before she started getting busy on the weekends too.’

If Nicola had been listening properly then she would have heard that her mother had been right. Nicola was six years old when she had been left with her neighbours next door while Colin went swimming, and it was mainly because Nicola didn’t have any weekend activities of her own to partake in at that age. That had been because Nicola was a child who had been more interested in solitary pursuits like drawing, writing stories, and playing with her dolls, loving to dress them up and move them around the dollhouse that gave her so much joy as a youngster. Or at least it used to give her joy.

Things had changed quickly as she had got older.

It had got to the point where almost all the colour and sound had drained out of the room for Nicola and so much so that she was failing to hear that her father was talking to her and trying to ask her if she would like another drink.

‘Nicola? Is anybody home?’

She suddenly snapped out of her trance and realised that everybody in the room was looking at her, presumably confused as to why she wasn’t answering her father. John saw her turn towards him, and that let him know that she was finally out of her daydream.

'I thought you'd seen this film before?' John chuckled when he saw that his daughter was back in the real world. 'You can't be that engrossed in it.'

'Er, yeah, I have,' Nicola mumbled back. 'Sorry, I was miles away then.'

'I'll say,' John said as he got out of his armchair and started to collect some of the empty champagne flutes from around the room. 'Right, time for a top-up.'

'Don't have too much,' Ruth warned her husband before he could leave the room. 'You've got a lot to help me with tomorrow, and I don't want you being hungover on Christmas Day.'

'I'll hardly be hungover on a couple of glasses of cheap champagne,' he retorted, and Colin and Charlotte laughed as Ruth adamantly denied that the champagne she had bought from the supermarket was cheap, even though it probably was because it had certainly tasted like it.

It was all good-natured jesting, and every member of the family was enjoying seeing Ruth and John teasing each other. Every member except Nicola, who continued to struggle with the news she had just been given.

That was why she suddenly got off the sofa and walked out of the room.

And it was also why she ignored everybody when they asked her where she was going.

4

A person's childhood bedroom can conjure up all sorts of emotions in the person who once called it their own. The place where a youngster first learns about having their own space, the need for privacy, and keeping their belongings neat and tidy is a special place, and the memories that are formed in that room can last a lifetime. It was no different for Nicola as she stood in her childhood bedroom now and looked around at the four walls that she was so familiar with, the walls that were the borders of the part of this house that she could always call her own.

But even though it was the same room that she had slept in as a child, it looked very different now. There were no longer any posters of boybands on the walls, nor were there shelves full of pop CDs or cupboards full of dolls. Instead, this room had been redecorated by her parents when Nicola had grown up and moved out of this house, the décor now making this the perfect spare bedroom for guests to stay in rather than it being kept as a shrine to the past. The walls were painted white, and understated artwork had taken the place of the posters. The shelves were cleared of CDs and now housed several paperback books, most of which would have been read by Ruth because Nicola's mum was the real reader in the family. And the cupboards that had once been filled with dolls that had brought Nicola so much joy had now been refitted into tall wardrobes where John kept most of his coats until guests came to stay, when they were given use of the storage space instead.

This room looked very different to how it had looked in the past, but Nicola didn't blame her parents for redecorating. Why would she? It was their house, and they could do what they wanted to with it. And besides, she hadn't called this place her permanent home since she was eighteen, just before she had gone off to study nursing at university. Nicola had been keen to get away from here and not just to meet new people and learn new things. She had wanted to get away, taking the opposite approach to her neighbour, Eric, who had remained here for most of those years, trying his own way at processing the pain of the past. Nicola hadn't even returned here fully after graduating, instead opting to move into a flat with a few friends even though she could barely afford it. But she hadn't cared, and her parents had been supportive of her plans, even if they might have secretly wished for a couple more years of having their daughter around the house.

But now Nicola was back, and while it was only for the Christmas holidays, it was evident that Ruth and John were loving having their children back under one roof again. The house was busy and full of noise, just like it had been back in Nicola and Colin's childhood, and it was certain to only get busier and noisier when they woke up on Christmas Day tomorrow. Nicola loved seeing her parents so happy and content to be surrounded by the family that they had created, or at least she had been until she had learnt about what had happened to Bill. That news had sent her off into a tailspin, and it was why she had retreated upstairs to her bedroom, seeking out a little privacy in the one place in this house where she had always been able to get it.

Sitting down on the edge of the bed that had once seemed so large to her but now just looked like a standard size, Nicola stared at the suitcase that was sitting on the carpet by her feet and thought about how she should really unpack her things. It wasn't like her to leave her clothes crumpled up in a suitcase when she arrived at her destination. She usually took the first opportunity she had to get her clothes on hangers in a wardrobe and put her toiletries in the bathroom by the sink, ready to be used when she needed them. But she hadn't done any of that since arriving here. Part of that was because she had been so excited to catch up with her family downstairs, but it was also because of something else.

It was because Nicola had seen Barbara on the way to this house, and it had knocked the younger woman off her stride.

Sitting on her old bed, Nicola thought about that old woman again now and, specifically, the fact that she had lost her husband this year. Nicola knew how long Bill and Barbara had been together, and she knew how much they loved each other. Therefore, there was no way the death of her husband had been anything other than devastating for the wife who had been left behind.

How was she coping with her loss? She had seemed okay when Nicola had just seen her out on the snowy street, but it had only been a brief encounter, and it hadn't told her much, other than that the old woman had been surprised to see Nicola. But after learning of Bill's sudden passing, Nicola wanted to know how Barbara had taken it and, most of all, how she was feeling right now. It was hard not to think of the elderly woman sitting all alone in that house next door, surrounded by photos and other memories of her late husband and feeling lonelier than ever before, particularly at this time of year.

Was Barbara okay, or was she depressed?

Had she moved on, or was she still wallowing in grief?

Could she learn to enjoy the later years of her own existence, or did she wake up every day now wishing she could join her beloved partner in the afterlife?

Nicola did not have the answers to those questions, and there was no real way for her to ever get them other than asking Barbara herself, but that was not something she wanted to do. What she did feel like doing was getting up off this bed and going to her bedroom window because she knew that from there, she would have a decent view of the house next door thanks to the way the top of this street was laid out.

Rather unusually, in comparison to most other streets, the houses on this one were all set back at different points rather than standing side by side in the traditional fashion. Barbara and Bill's house was a little behind Nicola's parents' home, and that meant she had always been able to get a good view of the neighbouring property whenever she had peeped out of her window as a youngster. But having left the bed and creating a gap in the curtains, Nicola was now peering out of the window as an adult.

The first thing Nicola noticed when she looked outside was how much more snow had fallen since she had arrived here. The entire back garden was blanketed in white powder, as were all the treetops and the roofs of the other houses that made up this quiet neighbourhood. It really did look quite beautiful, and Nicola would have been more than happy to just stand and admire the view if it wasn't for the fact that she had something much more pressing that she wanted to look at.

Moving her eyes away from the winter wonderland all around her, Nicola focused on the house next door and noted that it looked rather dark apart from one pale light that was on in a downstairs window. Nicola knew from her times inside that house that the room with the light on was the living room, and it was where the two armchairs were located, the furniture positioned side by side so that Barbara and Bill had always been able to sit near to each other when they had watched TV or read a book.

Nicola assumed that Barbara was in that room now, considering that it was the only one with a light on, and because of that, she imagined her sitting alone, the chair beside her vacant and never to be filled again. Perhaps that room was filled with the sounds from the TV, or maybe it was deadly quiet, the only sound coming from that ticking Grandfather clock that always used to spook Nicola out whenever she was left alone to listen to it when her parents had taken her brother swimming.

Other than the light glowing on the other side of the curtains that were pulled across the living room window, there were no other signs of life in that house. There were certainly no Christmas decorations on display on the front of the property, nor were there any of the flashing lights that many of the other neighbours around here had decided to add to the exterior of their homes to show that they were very much in the festive spirit. To an outside observer, it would appear that there was a distinct lack of Christmas spirit at Barbara's house, and it was hard to argue otherwise. Nicola wondered if the elderly homeowner had even bothered to put a tree up in her home this year. Maybe she hadn't bothered on account of the fact that she would be the only one who would get to see it, so what was the point? But then Nicola recalled that Barbara and Bill had a son and that he could be home with his mother for the holidays.

Tony was his name. Was he back for Christmas? It was possible, but Nicola doubted it because she knew that Tony had learning difficulties and the last she had heard, he had been living in sheltered accommodation with other people like him. Nicola's dad had told her about Tony's living situation before she had moved to Australia and about how the decision had been made because Barbara and Bill had been getting too old to be able to sufficiently look after their son's needs all of the time. That might have sounded like a shame, but Nicola knew otherwise.

She knew Tony was better off out of that house.

Nicola was almost too busy daydreaming to notice that a small gap had appeared in the centre of the drawn curtains of the house next door, and that suggested somebody was looking outside just like she was. But Nicola leapt away from her window when she did notice, and as she closed her own curtains, she prayed that she hadn't just been seen spying.

'Nicola! Your brother's going!'

The call upstairs from John forced Nicola even further away from the window and out of her room to the top of the staircase, where she looked down to see Colin, Charlotte, and Ben with their coats on, ready to leave.

Nicola went down the stairs to give them a better goodbye than she could offer by staying up there, and the first person she went to say farewell to was the six-year-old who had almost disappeared beneath a bundle of hats, scarves, and gloves.

'Bye, Auntie Nicola,' Ben said as she crouched down to her nephew and welcomed him into a warm hug.

'See you tomorrow, Ben,' Nicola replied. 'And be good for your mummy and daddy tonight so that Santa comes to see you.'

Ben looked extremely excited about the prospect of a visit from Father Christmas sometime during the night, and it was a reminder of how this time of year really is all about the children.

'It's kind of nice to have you back. See you tomorrow, sis,' Colin said as he gave Nicola a hug, and that was another reminder, this time that the two siblings cared for each other a lot more than their constant teasing of each other would suggest.

After bidding Charlotte farewell, Nicola joined her parents in the doorway of their house as they watched their other family members get into their car to make the short drive back to their house. Colin and his family only lived ten minutes away, and they would be back here tomorrow for Christmas dinner, but Ruth and John still waved them off as if they were departing on a huge voyage and wouldn't be returning for many months yet.

It was freezing cold with the front door open, and Nicola longed to return to the warmth of her bedroom, so she told her parents that she was going to have an early night, pretending like she was tired from her train journey rather than telling them the truth, which was that she just wanted some more time by herself.

John and Ruth had no problem with her plan, mainly because they had a lot to do to sort out the preparations for the big meal they would all be enjoying tomorrow, so they wished their daughter goodnight before scurrying into the kitchen and losing themselves in all the potato peeling and place setting they had to do.

Returning to her bedroom, Nicola did what she should have done a few hours ago, unpacking her things and making herself more at home before finally being able to turn out the light and crawl under the duvet. As she lay there on her back in the darkness, she stared up and waited for her eyes to adjust so that she would be able to make out the details of the ceiling above her. When she could, she was able to read the words that she had written on this ceiling with a glow-in-the-dark pen that she had 'borrowed' from school after a science lesson in which the teacher had explained exactly why the ink in that pen was only visible with the lights turned off.

The glowing words on the ceiling of this otherwise dark bedroom became more readable the longer Nicola's eyes adjusted to the light in here, and it wasn't long until she could read the message clearly, not that she needed to see it to know what it said. She was the one who had written it after all, but she still liked to read it because it was a reminder of what she had been thinking at the time she had scribbled it onto this ceiling after scrambling up onto a chest of drawers and reaching up as far as her short arms would allow.

'It's not my fault.'

That sentence might have seemed like a fairly heavy thing for a young girl to write on her bedroom ceiling, and it was, but nobody really knew the true meaning behind it apart from the person who had written it. The fact that the message was only visible when the lights were out in this room meant that it had been many years later before anyone other than Nicola had read it, and by that time, the author of the message had left home and was working as a nurse in adulthood. It was John who noticed it first, having spent a night sleeping in this room after a particularly boozy evening at the local pub, after which Ruth had told him that him and his snoring were not welcome in her bed that night. Nicola's father had called his daughter the next day and asked her about the words on the ceiling, namely when she had written them and what they meant. Nicola had told him the truth that she had written the message when she was a young girl, but she hadn't been honest when she had told her dad that she had been bullied for a short while at school, and that had been why she had created the message.

She had told him that it was a visual reminder to herself to not let other people get the better of her feelings and emotions, and while John had been shocked to learn that his daughter had apparently been bullied, Nicola told him it had only been a minor thing and that it really wasn't that big of a deal.

But it was, or at least the real truth was.

It was a very big deal.

Staring up at those illuminated words above her head, Nicola felt a single tear run from the corner of her left eye and down her cheek before it hit the pillow beneath her head. It was no different to all the tears she had cried before while looking up at this message because it carried just as much pain as those times that had gone before it. The only difference was that she was better at composing herself quicker in adulthood than she had been as a child, so she wiped her eyes before rolling over on the mattress and staring at the wall instead of the ceiling.

As she lay there alone in the bed, the touching words still visible above her if she dared to look up again, Nicola felt as lonely as she had felt all those years ago, and that was despite being back home with her family. It made no sense for her to feel lonelier here than she had done on the other side of the world, yet that was exactly how she felt.

Her parents had already tentatively broached the subject with her tonight about whether or not there might be a man waiting for her back in Australia, perhaps one that they might one day get to call son-in-law. But Nicola had quickly dismissed that notion and told them there was nothing to report as far as her love life went. Thankfully, her parents knew better than to keep prying, and they had left it at that, seemingly happy enough as long as their daughter was happy.

But Nicola wasn't happy, and that was because she longed to have a partner to share her life with. A man sleeping beside her in this bed right now. An arm wrapped around her waist as she drifted off. Somebody she could love and trust and grow old with.

Like her mother and father had.

Like Colin and Charlotte had.

And like Barbara and Bill had before he died.

Christmas was no time to be alone. But that was not an option for Nicola. She couldn't see how she could ever let somebody in enough to have that kind of company with another man. The closest she had come had been last year when she had been dating one of the doctors whom she had met at the hospital at which she was employed in Sydney.

He had been a good man.

But things had ended very badly between them.

5

ONE YEAR EARLIER

The restaurant for this evening's date had clearly been chosen with one thing in mind.

To impress.

Well, it had worked, Nicola thought as she stared out of the window beside her table at the lights belonging to the Sydney Harbour Bridge and the glow of the Opera House just a short way across the water from that huge feat of engineering.

This venue easily had one of the best views available to any diner in Australia, and Nicola was struggling to concentrate on the food in front of her, such was the awe-inducing nature of the scenery she overlooked. Not that the items on her plate were anything to be sniffed at either.

It wasn't every day that she got to eat lobster.

The waiter tasked with serving Nicola's table this evening had already spent five minutes very politely informing her on the best way to eat the large crustacean in front of her before her date had spent a further five demonstrating what she had just been told. Now Nicola felt like she was getting the hang of it, but she was still taking her time so that she didn't embarrass herself. Furthermore, she didn't want to make it even more obvious that she was out of her depth in a place as prestigious as this one, where the drinks prices were almost as staggering as the view.

The man sitting across the table from her was plainly accustomed to dining in these types of restaurants and paying these kinds of prices, but then again, he was one of the top surgeons at the hospital where Nicola worked. But she was just a nurse, which meant her salary was less impressive than his, and while she was still earning a lot more than she did back in the UK, it wasn't as if lobster and champagne were things she could treat herself to very often. Sure, she could afford to eat here with her last paycheque, but only if it meant not eating anything else for the rest of the month.

'You're doing well,' Harrison, the fine-dining doctor, said after observing Nicola successfully consume another part of her lobster without making as much of a mess as the first time she had tried it.

'Thanks,' Nicola mumbled back with a mouthful of food before silently cursing herself for her bad table manners.

Looking around the restaurant, Nicola didn't see anybody else in here struggling with their food or talking with their mouths full. They were all the picture of prestige, eating easily, talking quietly, and sipping their drinks with an ease that suggested this was just another Friday night in Sydney for them. But this was not a typical Friday night for the nurse sitting by the window. This time of the week usually consisted of Nicola sitting on the sofa in her apartment and watching some British TV shows on her laptop with a glass of wine and a takeaway from a place that definitely did not serve anything as classy as lobster. But that fact had nothing to do with her financial situation, nor her lack of friends to socialise with. Instead, it was a choice. She tended to stay in more than go out on the weekends when she wasn't contracted to work because that way, she knew she wouldn't be approached by any guys looking to take her out on dates.

But while that had worked for her up to a point, she hadn't been able to avoid the advances of all men because she still had to go to work, and it was there where Harrison, the hunky doctor from the Oncology Department, had first approached her. Nicola had seen him around her workplace before, usually in the staff canteen when she had been grabbing a quick bite to eat in the middle of yet another hectic shift. But he had apparently noticed her too, and when he had sat himself down at her table one afternoon, Nicola realised he hadn't just noticed her, but he had also made up his mind to ask her out on a date.

Perhaps it had been the surprise of the encounter in that canteen, or maybe it was just because she felt too awkward to turn down the advances of a guy she would have to regularly see at work, but Nicola had accepted the invitation to go for a coffee with Harrison the following week. That first date had seen Nicola wake up with butterflies in her stomach, but it wasn't nerves about what could have been the first day of a budding romance. Instead, it had been the nerves that she always felt whenever she started letting a guy get close to her. She felt those nerves because she always knew how it was going to end, and it never ended well.

But that coffee date had gone well, so well, in fact, that Nicola had almost forgotten about her emotional and physical baggage and found herself having fun as if she was just a normal woman and not the mess she knew she really was. The date had taken place on a sunny spring day in Sydney, and the weather had been as crisp and calm as the conversation, with the sky as blue as the smart shirt Harrison had worn to impress Nicola.

The nurse had found herself having no trouble finding things to talk about with her suitor, their shared experiences in the world of hospitals and patient care giving them plenty in common to get started before they had moved on to more personal topics like where each of them hailed from. Nicola had told Harrison about the town in England that she called home, and while he hadn't heard of it, Harrison at least did a good job of pretending like it was just as impressive a place to come from as where he did, which it most certainly wasn't. That was because Harrison hailed from Port Douglas, a coastal town in Far North Queensland which Nicola knew as one of the best places to go to take a boat trip out to see The Great Barrier Reef.

The impressed nurse wasn't quite sure how her hometown could ever compete with a place so close to one of the world's seven natural wonders, but she did give it a good go, mentioning that her place of birth was famous for being the home of one of the largest biscuit factories in Europe. Harrison had laughed at that claim to fame before asking her if she thought her hometown attracted more visitors per year than his, and Nicola had to admit that it was unlikely, but given the choice, she would prefer a packet of biscuits over a day trip out on the Reef any day.

That sense of humour had obviously appealed to Harrison because he had ended their first date by suggesting they go on a second one. Things had gone so well that Nicola could find no good reason to say no, or not one she could voice honestly anyway, so the next date had been set.

Friday night at the seafood restaurant overlooking the harbour. It was perfect.

Or at least it would have been if Nicola hadn't known she had made a big mistake in coming here.

Despite the spectacular setting and the lovely company, Nicola knew it had been a mistake to agree to another date. It was a mistake because she knew things couldn't go any further, so there really was no point in leading Harrison on. He was a lovely man, and a guy like him would surely have no trouble finding somebody else to sit across this table from him and share a meal and a bottle of champagne with. But he was wasting his time with his current date. He just didn't know it yet, and that was Nicola's fault because she hadn't made it clear. She was leading him on by laughing at his jokes, answering his questions, and thanking him whenever he gave her another compliment, and the more this went on, the harder she knew it would be to let him down when the time came.

But there was no alternative. She would have to let him down. All she could hope was that he would take it well. The best-case scenario would be that he would remain the perfect gentleman and walk away into the night, disappointed but understanding of her wish to not take their interactions any further. The worst-case scenario would be that he would call her a tease, lament the fact that he had spent so much on this dinner, and then demand that she give him some money back before storming away and ensuring that it would be very awkward when they next saw each other at the hospital.

It remained to be seen which scenario played out.

The rest of the date went as well as what had gone before it, and Nicola greatly enjoyed the fact that her dessert was much easier to eat than her main course had been. It was a shame about having to leave the special view from the restaurant behind as they walked away from their table in the direction of the exit, but as it turned out, Harrison wasn't done treating Nicola on that front yet.

No sooner had the pair left the restaurant by the water then they were walking along the edge of the harbour as the doctor promised to show his date his favourite spot to see this spectacular location. The well-fed duo chatted about how lucky they both felt to live in such a desirable city as this one and how they felt like they would struggle to find anywhere else that could ever compare to Sydney if they were to move and work elsewhere. But neither of them had any plans to pack up their bags and hit the road, and that was just one more thing that boded well for the potential of this budding relationship.

Yet it still remained a relationship that Nicola knew was doomed to fail.

'Here we go,' Harrison suddenly said after a brief moment of silence that wasn't at all awkward. 'What do you think?'

He gestured towards the water beside them, and Nicola only had to look up for a split second to see that her date really had been right in telling her this place had the best view in the city. Somehow this vantage point topped the one that they had been treated to in the restaurant, and coupled with the warm breeze in her face from another mild Australian evening, Nicola felt as good as she could remember feeling in a long time.

It was clear that Harrison had pulled out all of the stops for her tonight, and normally, such endeavours should be rewarded, at least with a kiss.

And it seemed that was exactly what the doctor had in mind at that moment.

Nicola was looking down at the water that was only a couple of yards away from them, just below the edge of the concrete platform that made up the edge of this harbour they were standing on. But she could see Harrison in her peripheral vision stood beside her, and he was looking more at her than of the view now. Another silence had fallen between them, and while this one wasn't awkward either, it felt different.

This wasn't a break in conversation before the next topic arose.

This was a break before the perfect opportunity for their first kiss.

As Nicola felt Harrison move a little closer towards her, she knew she needed to say or do something that could at least delay the inevitable.

'I bet you bring all the girls here, don't you?' she jested, and while it might not have been exactly what Harrison had in mind as the perfect moment for romance was tempered slightly, he didn't falter and was still relaxed enough to see the humour in the remark.

'Only the ones who know how to eat a lobster,' he replied with a grin, and Nicola smiled, but she wished she could have laughed because that was what his joke deserved. But laughing was only something that a relaxed, happy person could do, and Nicola could not describe herself as either of those things. On the surface, she might have appeared as calm as the water beside them, but inside, she was a mess of jangling nerves and regret.

She was nervous about what might happen next.

And she was regretting letting things get this far.

Reaching out towards her face, Harrison attempted to tuck a strand of Nicola's hair back behind her ear from where it had fallen out of place on her head, but the kindly gesture had its moment ruined somewhat by the fact that Nicola flinched before the caring doctor could complete his task.

'I'm sorry,' he said when he realised he had caused the nervous reaction from his date.

'No, I'm sorry,' Nicola replied quickly, attempting to laugh it off but unsure if she was making up for it by doing so. After all, there surely weren't many men who enjoyed making their prospective partner startled in what should have otherwise been a romantic moment.

Harrison smiled to show that there was no harm done, and as he stared into Nicola's eyes, he told her how beautiful she looked in the light of the harbour. It was a lovely compliment and one that deserved a thank you, but Nicola failed to say anything. She just smiled weakly and averted her gaze from his face to the water beside them in a move that could be taken as a sign of shyness rather than the fear that was really behind it.

Then it happened.

Harrison went in for a kiss.

But Nicola pulled away.

'I'm sorry,' Harrison said quickly when he realised his smooth moment hadn't gone as smoothly as he had anticipated.

'No, it's okay,' Nicola told him, but the disappointment was evident on the doctor's face, and it would take some story to convince him that she wasn't actually as repulsed by him as her actions had just made out.

'I just thought things were going well,' Harrison told her.

'They were. I mean they are! It's just…'

Nicola's voice trailed off as it often did in moments like these throughout her life when it came to the crucial time of deciding whether to be honest with a prospective male partner or whether to just turn and run as fast as she could in the opposite direction.

'What's wrong?' Harrison asked her as if she was a sickly patient who had turned up in his office desperately seeking a diagnosis. He looked genuinely concerned, and while that was sweet, Nicola wasn't looking for sympathy or pity. But she knew she would get plenty of it if she was honest and told him the truth.

That's why she couldn't do it.

But she also knew that she couldn't keep going on like this. Letting perfectly good men get as close to her as possible before the point where she would dash their hopes and leave them both alone was not only cruel but completely pointless. Something had to change unless she wanted to be alone forever, which she definitely did not. Either she had to start confiding in men like Harrison, or she just had to force herself to become comfortable getting closer to them in the hope that she could keep her past buried down deep below.

Neither of those options were ideal, but one of them did seem slightly easier than the other, which was why Nicola went with that one in the end.

Looking Harrison in the eyes again, Nicola apologised for a second time about the awkward moment she had just caused between them before offering a weak smile and trying to make it clear that she was okay if he wanted to try again with the kiss.

It took the doctor a couple of seconds to catch on to her line of thinking, but when he did, he smiled and moved in closer, closing his eyes at the split second before his lips met hers.

Nicola forced herself to close her eyes too, even though her instincts were telling her to keep them open for this intimate moment, and as they kissed, the

Englishwoman was suddenly reminded of everything she had been denying herself of for so long.

The connection with another human being.

The pleasure.

The passion.

And the pain.

Despite her best efforts, Nicola was unable to keep her demons at bay, and she attempted to break off from the kiss. But Harrison was very much into it and didn't realise that she was wanting to stop, so he didn't draw back his head and give her a little space. He just kept kissing her. And the more he did, the more agitated Nicola felt herself becoming.

That was the only explanation for why she did what she did next.

She pushed him away from her as hard as she could, her hands hitting his chest and driving him backwards towards the harbour's edge and causing the startled doctor to flail out his arms as he grasped at thin air for something to keep him upright.

But there was nothing, and despite realising with horror what was about to happen, Nicola could only watch on with her hands over her mouth as she saw the doctor fall into the water that had provided the stunning backdrop to the majority of their date this evening.

It was dangerous.

It was a disaster.

And it was just another reminder to Nicola that she could still not allow anybody to get too close to her.

6

PRESENT DAY

Waking up on Christmas morning used to be a magical experience for Nicola.

As she lay in her bed in adulthood, the woman fondly recalled those delightful days when she would open her eyes as a child on December 25th and wonder if Santa Claus had been kind enough to pay her a visit. The way to find out if that was the case had been to quickly crawl down to the bottom of the bed and feel the stocking that hung on her bedpost.

If it was empty, then he hadn't been. But it was never empty.

It was always big and bulky, and that meant there were presents inside.

Nicola stared up at her ceiling as she visualised herself running down the stairs as a young girl alongside her brother with their parents behind, camera in one hand and a big grin on their faces as they prepared to see their children's dreams come true. Rushing into the living room, the youngsters would catch a glimpse of all of the presents sitting beneath the Christmas tree, and that was easily the best moment of any child's year.

Tearing open the wrapping paper with wild abandon, various toys would emerge. Dolls. Diggers. Games. Trains. And sweets. Lots and lots of sweets. Nicola and her older sibling would spend the rest of that morning in their dressing gowns, playing with their new possessions and stuffing their faces with sugary foods despite their mother warning them not to spoil their dinner later. But the fact that they had eaten so much never seemed to spoil their enjoyment of the turkey and the gravy, just like the fact that they had been up since the crack of dawn never seemed to make them tired enough to need their beds later in the day.

They never got tired on Christmas Day.

There was simply too much fun to be had.

Nicola almost longed for those innocent times again when Christmas felt more like a fairytale and less like the busy, sometimes stressful day it tended to be in adulthood. She only almost longed for it because as good as those youthful days were, they were also accompanied by the beginnings of a dark period in Nicola's life, and there was no way she ever wanted to relive that.

Picking up her phone from her bedside table, Nicola saw that it was 09:26. Christmas morning was almost halfway through, and she hadn't even gotten up yet, which was just another reminder of how her feelings about this day had changed over the years. Listening out for any other noises in the house, she heard some movement in the kitchen downstairs and figured it was caused by her parents, who were up early to make sure dinner was being cooked to its strict schedule. But they had surely enjoyed more of a lie-in too this morning, no longer required to get up when their children came bounding into their bedroom with excited cries about how Father Christmas had been and eaten the cookies that had been left out for him in the hallway.

Letting out a weary groan that she seemed to have adopted as part of her morning routine at some point in her thirties, Nicola pulled back the duvet and put her bare feet down on the carpet. No longer needing to check for a stocking at the bottom of her bed, she instead just stood up and stretched before making her way into the bathroom to have a shower and get herself ready to start the day.

By the time she was dressed and ready to make an appearance downstairs, she could hear Christmas music playing in the kitchen and the whistle of her father as he seemingly enjoyed the early part of what promised to be a pleasant day spent with his loved ones. It was heartwarming for Nicola to hear his happiness, but as she reached the bottom of the stairs and prepared to enter the kitchen, it was also a reminder of her own distinct lack of it.

She couldn't remember the last time she had whistled. In fact, she couldn't recall ever doing it because by the time she had been old enough to know how to do it, she had not felt like making such a cheerful noise.

'Merry Christmas,' Nicola said as she arrived in the kitchen and saw her parents standing over a busy stove full of pots and pans that were filled with vegetables, only some of which Nicola liked enough to want to put on her plate later.

'Merry Christmas, love!' Ruth cried as she put down a spoon and rushed towards her daughter to give her a hug.

Despite being closer to forty than four, Nicola's Mum still acted as though this day of the year was as special for her child as it had always been.

John was slightly more restrained with his greeting, and after wishing his daughter a Merry Christmas, he asked if she would like a glass of Buck's Fizz, to which Nicola replied that she would.

Taking a seat at the breakfast bar and sipping the glass of champagne and orange juice she had just been handed, Nicola watched her parents work as the Christmas songs continued to play on the radio. The DJ's setlist consisted of all the usual tracks that tended to surface at this time of year, from *Fairytale Of New York* to *Do They Know It's Christmas Time,* and Nicola was just enjoying the opening chords of *Rockin' Around The Christmas Tree* when she realised that she should probably offer to help her parents with some of the many jobs that needed doing before Christmas dinner was ready and the rest of their family arrived.

'What can I help with?' she asked as she got up out of her seat and joined her parents by the hot stove and even hotter oven, inside which were a tray of pigs in blankets that looked good enough to eat right now, even if they weren't fully cooked yet.

'You could finish setting the table if you don't mind,' John suggested, and Nicola was happy enough to do that, so she left the busy kitchen and the Christmas music behind to go into the dining room and check on the state of the table that would accommodate the mountain of food that was currently being prepared.

Getting a first glimpse of the table, Nicola saw that there didn't seem to be too much left to do. The cutlery was already out and positioned in front of each chair, the place settings forming the foundation around which everything else on this table would be built. But there were no napkins out yet, nor were there any Christmas Crackers, so Nicola went into the cupboard behind the table and had a look around for what she required.

Finding a small stack of napkins alongside a large box of crackers, Nicola got to work putting out the additional items at each place setting in as tidy a fashion as she could because otherwise, her mother would only go around after her and rearrange it all. After finishing putting out the napkins and crackers, Nicola stepped back and checked the table again to quickly count out what she had done and make sure she hadn't missed anything. But it was then that she realised something.

There were six people attending this meal.

But there were seven place settings.

Counting again to make sure that she hadn't made a mistake, Nicola was able to confirm that there really was an additional place setting to the number she had been expecting, so that was why she left the dining room and went back into the kitchen to enquire.

'Why is the table set for seven?' she asked her parents as another festive song blared out, and the heat from the pans continued to steam up the windows in here.

'Oh, we must have forgotten to mention it to you,' John said as he picked up a sack of potatoes and dropped it onto the countertop. 'We've invited Barbara for Christmas dinner.'

The shock of that statement, combined with the noise and the heat in the room, caused Nicola to feel as though she needed to steady herself by grabbing the edge of the breakfast bar beside her.

'What?' she uttered when she had composed herself.

'We invited Barbara,' Ruth casually confirmed as she handed her husband a peeler so that he could get to work on skinning the potatoes. 'She was going to be on her own, so we thought it would be nice to invite her to have Christmas dinner with us. Sorry, we thought we'd told you.'

'No, you didn't tell me!' Nicola cried, and the pain she suddenly felt in her right hand told her that she was now gripping the breakfast bar with increasing anxiety. But that was nothing compared to the swarm of sensations that were rushing through the rest of her body.

'Sorry, love. But it's not a problem, is it?'

'Yes, it is!'

'Why?'

Ruth and John both stopped what they were doing and looked up at their daughter, waiting for her answer while *I Wish It Could Be Christmas Every Day* played in the background, making this dramatic moment seem a little less tense, at least from their point of view anyway. But it was still very much a serious moment for Nicola but not just because she had found out their elderly neighbour would soon be joining them. It was because she now had to come up with a reason why it wasn't a big problem for her.

'Erm…' she said, stalling for time as her parents waited for an explanation. 'Because it's supposed to be a family meal!'

That seemed to be a good enough excuse, and Nicola felt relieved she had been able to come up with something under pressure, but despite that, it didn't seem it was a good enough reason to protest.

'Try and see things from her point of view,' John said. 'How would you like it if you were on your own at Christmas?'

'What about her family?'

'She's only got Tony, but he's staying in the care home this year,' Ruth replied before going back to the task at hand, which in her case was putting a pre-made dessert back in the fridge. 'So she would have been all alone next door.'

'So? It's not our fault, and it shouldn't ruin our Christmas.'

'Nicola! It's not going to ruin our Christmas!' Ruth cried, seemingly shocked that her daughter would suggest such a thing. 'Why would you say that?'

But Nicola couldn't answer that one, so she kept quiet, allowing her father to re-enter the debate.

'What's the big deal with having her here for dinner?' John asked. 'We've all known Barbara for years. We get on well. Okay, so we might not all be quite as relaxed as we would be if it was just family, but inviting her over so she isn't by herself is the right thing to do. Don't you think?'

'I don't know.'

'Well, we've invited her, so it's too late to go back now,' John said, shaking his head and making a start on peeling the potatoes.

'But....' Nicola started, but Ruth closed the fridge and cut her daughter off before she could say another word.

'Honestly, I can't believe you have got a problem with this,' she said. 'I thought I'd raised you to be a little more caring than that.'

'You did! This isn't about not caring!'

'Then what's it about?'

Ruth waited for another answer from her daughter, but again, Nicola had the same problem that she had before in that she couldn't just tell the truth. If she did that then it wouldn't just be Christmas dinner that was ruined. *It would be everything.*

'What about Colin?' Nicola asked, remembering her brother and hoping he might be on her side in all of this. 'What has he said about this plan?'

'He's not got a problem with it. Why would he?'

'I don't know. Because it's just going to be awkward!'

'Why would it be awkward? You've both known Barbara since you were little. She's a sweet lady who is unfortunately on her own, just like me or your father might end up being one day. And I'd like to think that you wouldn't just leave us by ourselves at Christmas time if one of us passed away. But maybe I'm wrong about that.'

'Of course you wouldn't be on your own.'

'Well, good! So then why is it okay for Barbara to be on her own?'

'I don't know!'

'Neither do I! So she's coming for dinner, and that's that!'

Nicola and Ruth were clearly on the verge of a major argument, which was perhaps why John wisely stepped in at that point to calm things down between the warring pair.

'Guys! Come on. It's Christmas. There will be no arguing in this house today,' he said, and the tension eased a little in the room, at least from Ruth's side anyway. But Nicola was still just as wound up as before, only now she knew she would only make things worse if she continued to demonstrate that. That was why she opted to leave the room before she said anything else, heading back upstairs to her bedroom, where she closed the door and leaned back against it, mulling over the shock of what had just occurred.

This can't be happening, she thought as she stood there and tried to calm her racing heart. *Barbara can't be coming here. I cannot sit at the same table as that woman.*

But no matter how long she stood there alone in her childhood bedroom, Nicola couldn't calm herself down, and only the sound of the doorbell downstairs snapped her back into the moment.

Who was that at the door? she thought. *Was it her? Was it Barbara?*

Nicola felt all the muscles in her body tightening up as she listened out to discover who the visitor was, but she was flooded with relief when she heard that it was just her brother and his family arriving.

The sound of her nephew's high-pitched voice filtered up the staircase and into Nicola's bedroom, and she could tell how excited the little boy was about the fact that it was Christmas Day, and he was arriving at his grandparent's house where surely even more unopened presents would be waiting for him. Nicola would have loved nothing more than to rush down the stairs and give him a big hug, wishing him a Merry Christmas and giving him the opportunity to tell her all about what Santa had brought him so far. But she didn't do that. Instead, she just remained in her bedroom with her back to the door, listening to the happy voices of her family downstairs and feeling just as disconnected from her loved ones as she had before.

'Nicola! Your brother's here!' John called up the stairs a moment later, and that was her cue to leave her bedroom and go to see her visiting family members. But she didn't do that, although she was at least able to move away from the door. She moved over to the bedroom window instead and looked outside, and when she did, there was only one thing she was interested in looking at. She was looking at the house next door. The house where Barbara was now, alone but not for long. Somehow, the old woman had been able to secure an invitation to Christmas dinner at this house today, and it was only a matter of time until she took her turn to knock on the door and enter this property.

That fact angered Nicola as much as it frightened her. It angered her because she knew that

Barbara must be aware of how difficult her presence was going to be for Nicola, yet she had still accepted the offer and agreed to be at the dinner table today. That was infuriating and was just another reminder of how there were very few lows that the old woman would stoop to in her life.

'You bitch,' Nicola said under her breath as she glared at the property next door, the one with no decorations and most likely no festive music playing on the radio inside. Why would it be? It was a cold home, devoid of all love, so it was no place for the kind of songs that families gathered around to listen to at this special time of year. If she had to guess, Nicola would say that Barbara was pottering around in that otherwise empty house now, counting down the minutes until it was time for her to put on her coat and walk next door. She wouldn't be doing anything else because she had nothing else to do.

No one to talk to. No one to share a drink with. Not even her son had bothered to come home for Christmas, and that said more about her than it did about him.

Nicola just wished Barbara would be spending the whole of today in that house instead of this one. But it seemed that was not an option. Barbara was going to come here whether Nicola liked it or not, and there was nothing she could do about it.

There was no doubt about it.

Nicola knew this was going to be the worst Christmas of her life.

7

Nicola had been nervously awaiting the next knock on the front door ever since finding out that her elderly neighbour would be joining her family for Christmas dinner. But it appeared that she need not have bothered because instead of Barbara being the one to come to them, it seemed that her father was going to go to her instead.

‘I’ll be back in a minute,’ John said as he put his coat on and headed for the door.

‘Where are you going, Grandad?’ Ben asked as he looked up from one of the many toys he had been gifted today to see one of his beloved grandparents preparing to leave the house.

‘I’m just going next door to get our neighbour,’ John replied.

‘Can I come?’ Ben wanted to know.

‘No, you stay here in the warm. I’ll only be a minute,’ came the reply before Nicola watched her father open the front door and step outside onto the snowy driveway.

Everybody in the warm house felt the blast of icy air when the door was open, so it was a relief when it was closed again because it really wasn’t a day to be spending any time outside. While the people of Britain might have got their wish for a white Christmas, the stunning snowy scene outside everybody’s home also made it almost impossible for anybody to get far from their front door today. Nicola could see from the windows that the roads were completely covered in a thick blanket of white powder, and the pavements weren't any better, meaning it would be extremely hazardous for anybody to try and venture out instead of staying inside where it was both warmer and safer. But John was doing what he believed to be yet another good deed by going next door to assist Barbara in making it safely to her neighbour's house for dinner, and it was a sign of how much of a gentleman Nicola's father really was. That should have warmed Nicola's heart, but it failed to do so in the circumstances. Instead, the thought of her dad linking arms with Barbara and making small talk with her as they both shuffled their way down the driveway only sent a shiver down her spine, and this one had nothing to do with the cold air getting in from outside.

Looking for something to busy herself with so that she didn't have to think about that or the fact that the old woman would be here very soon, Nicola sat down beside Ben and asked him what he was playing now.

'Soldiers,' came the response from the young boy, and Nicola smiled as she watched him pretend to create a battle between several of his figurines whilst making lots of noises that she presumed were supposed to represent all the guns and explosions going off.

Sitting beside her nephew as he revelled in the joys of Christmas Day made her feel like making the long trip over from Australia to be here with him today had been worth it, but there was another reason why she felt glad that she was back. It was because as much as she would hate having her in this house, Nicola would be able to keep an eye on Barbara now that she was home instead of in Australia. As much as she despised her next-door neighbour, Nicola took some solace in the fact that things might have seemed a lot worse if she had learned that Barbara was attending her family's Christmas meal without her present. That would be because she would only be able to imagine what was happening, and that would surely be worse than being here herself to keep tabs on it all.

As the famous saying said, *keep your friends close and your enemies closer.*

It took a surprisingly long time for the front door to reopen again and for John to reappear with Barbara by his side, but that was presumably because of how long it was taking them both to make it down the snowy driveway. But there was no delaying the inevitable, and when Nicola heard the door handle turning, she looked up even quicker than her nephew did to see who was coming inside.

'I'm back!' John called out as he re-entered his home before he turned and held out his hand for the old woman behind him to take. Barbara gratefully accepted the polite offer and used her neighbour's support to step off the snowy doorstep and onto the much less treacherous carpet inside the house, and as she moved further inside, Nicola got another good look at the woman she had spent most of her life hating.

While she had seen Barbara yesterday out on the street when they had briefly passed her in the car, it had been gloomy out there. That poor lighting coupled with the fact that Nicola had spent more time looking straight ahead instead of at the woman by her car window meant that she hadn't really got a proper look at the old woman, but she was definitely getting that now in the light of the hallway. And when she did, Nicola realised just how much Barbara had aged since the last time she had seen her.

Not only were the wrinkles on her face much deeper than before, but her movements were stiffer, her shoulders hunched, and her head bowed low as she shuffled deeper into the house with the aid of a walking stick that hadn't been present yesterday. Nicola wondered why she was using a stick today and not yesterday but assumed it was to provide extra support in the snow that had fallen in the meantime. Whatever the reason, the addition of the stick made Barbara look very frail, and as she clutched it with one of her wrinkled hands, Nicola almost found it hard to believe that this woman had once been as youthful as her.

But despite her advancing years and waning physical appearance, Nicola knew not to be fooled by the weary woman entering her family home. That was because no number of wrinkles, grey hairs, and walking sticks could change what this person had done in her past and because of that, there would be no sympathy extended from the younger woman towards the older one today. But the same could not be said for Nicola's other family members, all of whom were visibly eager to ensure that Barbara was okay and taken care of as she loitered by the door and looked around the home.

'Let me get your coat,' John said, ever the gentleman, proving that chaperoning Barbara from her front door to his own was not the only kindly act he was willing to do for her today.

'Hi Barbara! Merry Christmas! Can I get you a drink?' Ruth asked when she saw her guest, and the old lady said that a cup of tea would go down a treat right now.

'Merry Christmas, Barbara! Are you well?' Colin asked her before she confirmed that she was and then asked him if he was getting taller or if she was getting shorter.

'I like your bag,' Charlotte said, noticing the handbag hanging off Barbara's wrist, and the neighbour smiled before letting her know where she had got it from.

At that point, there were only two people who hadn't spoken since Barbara had entered the home. Nicola and Ben. But while the six-year-old could probably be excused for not speaking up and being a little shy in the presence of a stranger, Nicola knew that on the face of it, she had no good reason for not welcoming the visitor in.

It seemed that a few of the other people present noticed that too because no sooner had John hung Barbara's coat over the edge of the banister, then he looked towards his daughter and raised his eyebrows in a gesture that could only have been done to summon her into action.

But Nicola was reluctant to go over to Barbara and say hello. She was quite happy to stay where she was, sitting on the carpet beside Ben, and to prove it, she looked back down at the little boy's toys and indicated to him that she was ready to watch him start playing again. But John obviously wasn't ready for them to carry on without saying hello to their guest, so he decided to play the good host and try and initiate a little conversation between those who hadn't spoken yet.

'You remember Nicola, of course,' John said. 'Our special guest all the way from Australia.'

'Oh yes, of course. We saw each other briefly yesterday,' Barbara said as she eyed Nicola on the floor a few yards away from where she stood. 'But it's only now I can see how good the sunshine has been to you. I'm very jealous, dear.'

Nicola would have liked nothing more than to keep her eyes lowered on Ben's toys, but she knew that would have looked incredibly rude, not to the old woman but to her father, who was standing beside Barbara. With that in mind, she forced herself to look up and at least acknowledge her neighbour, who had just spoken to her before mumbling out a 'Merry Christmas' that was done solely to appease her dad and no one else.

Noticing that her father appeared to be a little puzzled by her distinct lack of interest in chatting with the woman who once babysat her, Nicola then forced a smile onto her face, but it was quickly wiped off a moment later when Barbara approached her and looked down at little Ben by her feet.

'Hello, dear. My, you have grown since the last time I saw you.'

Ben looked up at the old lady who had just spoken to him, and he seemed nervous, which was why his mum quickly came over to let him know that it was okay.

'This is your grandparents' next-door neighbour. You've met before, remember?' Charlotte said to her son. 'Say hello, Ben.'

'Hello,' the little boy mustered, and Barbara smiled, which was more than could be said for Nicola, who had resorted to glaring at the elderly woman again and wishing that she would take a few steps away.

'How old are you now, dear?' Barbara asked Ben, and after another prompt from his mother, he felt confident enough to answer her.

'Six.'

'Six! Oh my goodness. You are a big boy, aren't you? But you're still not quite as old as I am.'

Charlotte chuckled politely at Barbara's self-deprecating comment, but Nicola did not, and Barbara noticed it.

'Do you know how old I am?' the old neighbour asked Ben, to which he shook his head. 'I'm seventy-three, which makes me sixty-seven years older than you. Can you believe that?'

Ben shook his head to show that he could not, and that was to be expected because not many children could comprehend what it was like for somebody to be so much older than them. The young boy spent most of his days with kids his own age at school, and even his grandparents were still relatively young. But Barbara was much older, and she seemed keen to reinforce that fact, which Nicola thought might be a tactic on her part to pacify everybody here and make herself seem less of a threat. But Nicola would not be fooled by the tactics, just like she wasn't fooled by her appearance.

This was still a woman to be feared, whatever her age.

It was just that nobody knew it but her.

Nicola felt much better once Ruth returned with a cup of tea and ushered Barbara over to one of the sofas to take a seat. That at least allowed Nicola to focus on Ben and try and forget for a moment that the neighbour was here. But that didn't last long because after sitting down, Barbara reached into her handbag and took out a wrapped present before informing Ben that it was for him.

The little boy was still clearly nervous around this woman he didn't know all that well, but that was tempered somewhat by the fact that he had another present to open, and as Barbara beckoned him over to her, Nicola knew she wouldn't be able to compete with that. It was no good telling Ben to stay with her and keep playing with his toys, not when he had a new one to become acquainted with, so that was why she didn't bother. But she followed Ben over to Barbara and watched closely as her nephew received the gift from the seemingly kindly neighbour.

'What do you say?' Colin asked his son as he and his wife watched Ben take the present.

'Thank you,' Ben said to Barbara like a polite young boy, and she beamed at him as she observed him sit back down on the carpet and then eagerly tear into the wrapping paper.

Nicola watched on with just as much interest, and as Ben removed the wrapping, she saw exactly what he had just been gifted.

And she did not like it one bit.

'What is it?' Ben asked as he examined the item in his hand.

'It's a hand puppet,' Barbara told him. 'Here, let me show you how to use it.'

Barbara reached out to take the gift back from Ben, and while he was initially reluctant to give it up after just claiming ownership of it, his mother advised him to do so.

Putting the puppet on her hand, Barbara then demonstrated how it worked, and what had previously been a basic, knitted gingerbread man suddenly came alive as its head and arms began moving, capturing Ben's attention and making him realise that this present might not be as dull as he first thought.

'See, you can make it move,' Barbara told Ben as she continued to wriggle her fingers, and everyone in the room watched her make various gestures with the puppet, all of which Ben enjoyed if the smile on his face was anything to go by.

The fact that everyone in the room was watching the moving gingerbread man meant that no one had seen Nicola's expression, but if they had looked at her then they would have seen that she was mortified. That was because Nicola hated puppets. And she hated them because of Barbara.

'Would you like to have a go?' Barbara asked Ben, and he nodded his head enthusiastically before she handed him the gingerbread man, and he put it onto his much smaller hand. Despite it being a little bit too big for him, Ben was able to operate it well enough to get some enjoyment out of it, and as he watched the gingerbread nodding his head on his hand, the young boy seemed very happy with his latest Christmas present.

'Thank you,' he said to Barbara without needing any prompting from his parents this time, and she told the young boy that he was more than welcome before sitting back in her seat and taking a sip of her tea.

She very much looked like she was making herself at home, and that only added to the anger that was building up inside Nicola as Ben continued to play with the puppet.

'Why don't we go back to playing soldiers?' Nicola asked as she attempted to distract her nephew and make him put the puppet down. But Ben was enjoying playing with the gingerbread man, so he just ignored her and carried on wriggling his fingers, and that was when Nicola noticed Barbara smiling at her.

'You used to love playing with puppets when you were his age,' she said to Nicola. 'Do you remember?'

Of course Nicola remembered because there was no way she could forget. But she didn't want to give the old woman the satisfaction of confirming that, so she just shrugged and made it look like she either didn't know or didn't care. But that answer wasn't good enough for Barbara, and she pressed on.

'Remember. You used to play with a couple when we would babysit you. Your favourite one was the red bear, wasn't it? What was his name again?'

Nicola knew exactly what the bear's name was, but she was never going to say it.

'Beatrice!' Barbara cried as if she had just suddenly recalled a long-lost memory. 'That was the bear's name, wasn't it?'

But Nicola wasn't prepared to answer that, nor was she prepared to stay here and listen to this woman talk about things in the past. That was why she rushed out of the room and headed upstairs, where she locked herself in the bathroom before anybody could stop her and see the tears in her eyes.

Leaning over the sink and breathing heavily, Nicola did her best to keep the tears at bay, but she couldn't manage it, and it wasn't long until she was properly sobbing, the teardrops dripping down the plughole beneath her face.

'Sis? Are you alright?'

The call from Colin on the other side of the bathroom door snapped Nicola out of it, and she wiped her eyes quickly before taking a deep breath and standing up straight.

'I'm fine!' she called back. 'I'll be down in a minute!'

That seemed to be a good enough answer because Nicola heard her brother descending the staircase a moment later, and she felt better knowing he was no longer on the other side of the door waiting for her to reappear. That gave her an extra few minutes to make sure the tears really had stopped, and after checking in the mirror to make sure that her eyes weren't bloodshot, she was ready to leave the bathroom.

No sooner had she done that then she heard the cry go out from her mother in the kitchen.

'Take your seats at the table. Dinner is served!'

8

Judging by the amount of food sitting on the table, an outside observer could be forgiven for thinking that Ruth had cooked for seventy people instead of just seven. But nobody was complaining as they took their seats and eyed up all the dishes of hot food, although there was one person at the table who had a grievance. That was Nicola, and as she looked across the sea of delicious food spread out in front of her, she saw Barbara smiling widely and continuing to make herself at home.

So much for a special Christmas dinner with her family. For Nicola, this was now just an ordeal to get through.

'Tuck in, guys!' Ruth ordered, and the men in her family didn't need telling twice as both John and Colin grabbed a spoon and started shovelling various tasty treats onto their plate. Ben was happy to be served his food by his mother, while Ruth made sure that Barbara was okay to help herself, which she was and proved so by spooning some peas onto her plate.

But Nicola just sat and watched everybody else claiming their food without making a move to get her own, which wasn't like her at all because she had been in this family long enough to know that being hesitant at the dinner table often only ever led to an empty stomach.

'Are you okay?' Charlotte asked her sister-in-law when she noticed she wasn't greedily grabbing the food like everyone else around her.

‘Yeah, I’m fine. I just need another drink,’ Nicola replied before getting up from the table and leaving the dining room. Once she was alone in the kitchen, Nicola took another moment to try and compose herself away from the prying eyes of anybody else before she opened the fridge and took out an unopened bottle of wine.

Pouring herself a generous measure, Nicola glugged down several mouthfuls of her drink before taking a deep breath and wondering how much alcohol she might have to consume to really take the edge off her nerves today. But there was surely no magic amount that would make her feel better because she had spent plenty of time trying to numb her pain in the past with various drinks, and none of them had done the job. All they did was leave her feeling even more anxious the next day, so it was a fool’s game, not that it ever stopped her from trying again and again.

Finishing her first glass and pouring another, Nicola knew she couldn’t spend the entirety of Christmas dinner just hiding in the kitchen, so she forced herself to return to the dining room and retake her seat opposite Barbara. If there was one good thing to come out of this extremely awkward dinner, then it was that her mother hadn’t seated her beside her elderly neighbour. John had been the one to be ‘lucky’ enough to be sitting beside Barbara, so Nicola tried to console herself with the fact that at least she didn’t have to be any closer to the woman than she already was.

After putting some hot food on her plate, Nicola’s mood was helped very slightly by how tasty the meal was, and as she ate and listened to the chatter of her family around her, Nicola figured she could just zone out, and maybe this dinner wouldn't be so bad after all. But any chance of slipping into a daydream was shattered when Ben asked Barbara a very personal question.

'Why aren't you having Christmas with your family?'

There was a moment where everybody else around the table stopped what they were doing and looked towards the little boy who had just asked the potentially awkward question, while Nicola glanced at Barbara to gauge her reaction to it. But before the old woman could answer, Charlotte stepped in and tried her best to deflect it.

'I'm sorry,' she said to Barbara.

'No, it's okay,' the neighbour replied before putting down her fork and turning towards Ben, who was seated at the other end of the table. 'It's good that your son is so inquisitive.'

Nicola noticed her nephew frown at that last word, probably because he had no idea what it meant, before Barbara gave him her answer.

'I would love very dearly to be spending Christmas with my own family,' she said. 'But not everybody is so fortunate as to have that opportunity.'

'Why?' Ben asked, the little boy's curiosity now driving the conversation around this dinner table.

'Mind your own business and eat your meal,' Colin told his son, but again, Barbara made it clear that she was willing to answer the child's questions.

'It's okay. I'm happy to talk about it,' she said before Nicola noticed the old woman glance at her to check if she was paying attention, which she was.

'This is my first Christmas without my husband, Bill,' Barbara admitted as everybody around the table stopped eating and gave the slightly sombre topic the respect it deserved.

'Where is he?' Ben asked, and this time, Barbara answered before either of his parents could pull him up for potentially prying too much.

'Bill passed away at the beginning of this year,' she told him.

'How?'

'Ben! That's enough!' Charlotte told her son, drawing the line at her child wanting to know such a thing.

'No, it's good that your son is willing to ask difficult questions,' Barbara told Charlotte with a warm smile. 'That confidence will serve him very well later in life.'

'How about I grab us some more roast potatoes?' John suddenly said, looking to change the subject by drawing everyone's attention to the fact that one of the bowls in the middle of the table was now almost empty. But as John left the room to go and retrieve more cooked potatoes from the kitchen, Barbara picked up the original conversation where it had left off.

'Bill died from a heart attack,' she told Ben.

'What's a heart attack?'

'It's something that can happen to older people,' Barbara told him. 'But you don't have to worry about it at your age.'

She smiled at Ben then to ease any worries he might have about this thing called a heart attack that he had just been told about. But Nicola saw the smile on Barbara's face and decided that she was going to have a go at wiping it off.

'Was he in pain before he died?' Nicola asked her neighbour, and that seemed to surprise those around the table even more than any of Ben's questions had.

'Nicola!' Ruth said, trying to remind her child of her manners just like Colin and Charlotte had been doing with theirs.

But Nicola wasn't six like Ben, so she didn't care about getting in trouble with a parent. She was an adult, and she would say whatever she felt like saying, however uncomfortable it might have been for the person tasked with answering the question. The more uncomfortable the better, as far as Nicola was concerned.

Barbara stared at Nicola across the table before she answered, and it seemed like this might be where she wanted to put the conversation to bed. But to everyone's surprise, she did end up answering, and when she did, she was brutally honest.

'Unfortunately, I'm afraid he was,' she said. 'It wasn't pleasant.'

Nicola had not been expecting Barbara to be so honest with her, assuming that she would have just lied and said Bill died peacefully, even if he hadn't. But she had been very open and raw, so much so that it had now made everyone around the table feel uncomfortable.

'I wonder where John is with those potatoes,' Ruth said, and she got up from the table to go and check on him, even though it was just an obvious ploy to remove herself from this awkward conversation for a moment.

But neither Nicola nor Barbara turned to watch her go, instead opting to keep staring at each other as if they were silently goading the other one to speak again about Bill's death. But it was little Ben who spoke next.

'Do you have any other family?' he asked, and that snapped Barbara out of her stare down with Nicola.

'Yes, I have a son. He's called Tony.'

'How old is he?'

'He's thirty-eight. The same age as your auntie.'

Barbara smiled at Nicola after referencing her, but Nicola did not smile back.

'Where is he?' Ben wanted to know as his parents returned to eating their meals, seemingly having given up on trying to stem the flow of their son's questions now.

'He doesn't live with me anymore,' Barbara admitted. 'He lives with some other people now.'

'His friends?'

'Yes, I suppose they are his friends. But that's not the only reason he is there.'

'Why?'

Ben was showing no sign of stopping his inquisition of the one person at the table he was unfamiliar with, but neither was Barbara showing any signs of wanting it to stop either.

'Tony requires looking after a little more than other people his age,' Barbara said, and Nicola thought that was a nice way of putting it. The way she remembered Tony, yes, he had learning difficulties, but he also had a bad temper and could be dangerous if he wasn't pacified in the right way.

'But why isn't he visiting you today?' Ben asked, which was a sweet question from a sweet little boy.

'He's having dinner with all his friends,' Barbara replied with a smile. 'But we will see each other soon.'

It was at that moment that John and Ruth returned to the room, the former carrying a newly filled bowl of roast potatoes, while Ruth was holding the bottle of wine that Nicola had opened earlier.

'Here we go, guys,' John said as he presented the replenished stocks while Ruth offered out more wine to those around the table who were old enough to partake. Nicola wasted no time in accepting another measure, and as she put her refilled glass to her lips, she studied Barbara and thought about what she had said about Bill.

The old man had been in pain when he died. *What a shame*, Nicola thought sarcastically. *If only I had been there to see it.*

The rest of the main course passed by with various topics of conversation that weren't anywhere near as probing and personal as what Ben had been asking Barbara, and by the time everyone had finished their meals and sat back in their chairs, there were plenty of satisfied smiles on faces.

'That was amazing. Cheers, Mum and Dad,' Colin said as he raised his glass of wine to his parents, and everyone else had to agree that it had been a fantastic meal. But like most families' Christmas dinners, it wasn't over yet.

'Okay, time for dessert,' John said as he started to pick up the empty dishes, and everybody else offered their assistance in clearing the table as quickly as possible so that the cakes and puddings could come out pronto. But as the dirty plates were put in the kitchen and Ruth opened the fridge to start taking out the desserts she had prepared earlier, Barbara suddenly put her hand to her head as if she had forgotten something.

'The lemon cheesecake I made!' she cried. 'I've left it in my fridge.'

'Oh, don't worry. We've got plenty of food here,' Ruth told her, but that didn't make Barbara feel any better about leaving behind her contribution to this meal.

'No, I'll go and get it,' she said as she turned and headed for the kitchen door.

'Seriously, it's fine,' Ruth tried. 'It was nice of you to make a cake, but we've got so much here already that I'm sure we'll manage.'

'No, no. It won't take me long to go and get it,' Barbara replied, and it was clear she was adamant on returning to her house and getting the cake, regardless of what anybody else said.

'I think you should stay here, Barbara,' John advised her as he glanced out of the kitchen window. 'That snow is getting heavier again.'

'I'll be fine,' she told him, which caused him to roll his eyes as he realised he wasn't going to be able to leave her alone to go out there by herself. He would have to accompany her to make sure that she was okay, which was a problem because he was in the middle of helping his wife get the other multitude of desserts ready.

'Nicola, could you go with her?' John suddenly asked his daughter when he noticed her just standing by the breakfast bar.

'What?' she asked when she realised what he had just said.

'Can you go with Barbara to get her cake? I'd do it, but I'm a bit busy here helping your mum.'

'I'm sure she can manage out there,' Nicola tried as she looked out of the window at all the snow that was coming down, but it wasn't a very convincing argument.

'Nicola! Just go with her,' John told his daughter, and his tone of voice suggested that he was starting to lose his temper with his daughter's attitude towards the guest in their home.

But Nicola didn't care about that. She would rather send Barbara out there into the snow on her own than do her a favour. That was until Barbara suddenly took in a sharp intake of breath, and when everyone went to check on her in the hallway, they found her leaning against the banister and clutching her left hip.

'Are you okay?' John asked her as she continued to grimace.

'Yes. It's my arthritis. It's the cold weather. But I'm not sure I can walk too far right now. Maybe Nicola could help me, like you suggested?'

Barbara looked up at Nicola, and while she wasn't smiling, the younger woman felt like the older one was deceiving them all. She was faking her pain, Nicola was sure of it. *But why?*

'Here are my keys,' Barbara said, holding them out towards Nicola. 'The cake is in the fridge. You remember your way around, don't you?'

Nicola did remember her way around Barbara's home from the days her parents would drop her off there, but that didn't mean she wished to go back there again. But before she could make the decision for herself, her dad made it for her.

'Sure, Nicola can do that,' he said. 'Now let's get you sat back down, Barbara.'

With that, he led the elderly lady back to the dining room where she could retake her seat while Nicola remained in the hallway, the keys to her neighbour's house in her hand and seemingly no way of getting out of this mission now without kicking up a huge fuss.

Looking out of the window, Nicola saw the house next door through the snowflakes that were falling in between this property and that one. That was when the shiver that ran through her body felt as cold as the inclement weather outside.

9

Closing the front door behind her, Nicola felt the wet snowflakes landing on the top of her head as she looked up the pure white driveway and tried to figure out the best way to walk. Everything was carpeted in snow, from the concrete to the flowerbeds, so it was difficult to know exactly where to place her feet to encounter the least amount of obstacles. But with visibility reduced and the temperature dropping by the minute, Nicola knew she was better just making a start rather than loitering out here for too long.

Putting one foot in front of the other and heading up the driveway, Nicola heard the snow crunching beneath her feet as she moved. But other than that, the street was silent, and it was no surprise because only a fool would dare venture out in this weather. Right now, everybody else in this town was sitting inside their warm, cosy home, tucking into their dinner or watching the festive programming on the TV. But Nicola was trudging through the snow on the way to the one place where she had never thought she would ever have to go again.

As she reached the top of the driveway, Nicola slipped and almost lost her footing, and it was only the lamppost beside her that prevented her from falling to the icy floor. Having grabbed the post for support, Nicola made sure her feet were standing on slightly less slippy ground before she felt confident enough to let go and start walking again. As she went, she pondered what might have happened if she had been adamant about not going next door to get the cake from Barbara's fridge.

Had that really been an option?

Could she have avoided this if only she had refused to do her neighbour the favour?

Possibly, but it would have been very difficult for her to give a valid reason why she was refusing to go next door. She certainly couldn't have told the truth about why she didn't want to go to this house, that was for sure. But as she reached the top of Barbara's driveway and looked down it at the dark house at the bottom, Nicola told herself that this wouldn't actually be that bad.

She was an adult now. She would be by herself. Bill and Barbara weren't inside.

Therefore, she was safe.

It was a lot harder to get down this sloping driveway next door than it had been to walk up her parents' one, and it took Nicola longer than she would have liked to negotiate it successfully. By the time she reached the front door, Nicola felt her back aching from where she had been tensing up her body while trying to stay upright on the snow, and it was just one more reason for her to curse the old woman who lived here as she put the key into the lock.

Taking a deep breath and resisting the urge to turn around and scurry back up the driveway, Nicola turned the key, and with the door unlocked, she was able to push it open and see inside the home.

As she peered inside, she saw that it was even gloomier in the hallway than it was on the street behind her, and she knew that she would feel a little better just as soon as she could locate the light switch on the wall that would brighten this place up.

Stepping through the front door and fumbling around on the wall, it took Nicola longer than she would have liked to find the switch. But when she did, she was extremely grateful to find that the lightbulb worked, and the yellow glow it gave off allowed her to see where she was going a lot better.

It also allowed her to see that she seemed to have stepped into some kind of time capsule.

Looking around at the décor in the hallway, Nicola felt as if she had been transported back to a time before she had even been born. The wallpaper, furniture, and overall style in this first part of the house seemed to be one that was more in keeping with the 1960's, and not the modern-day style that Nicola was more accustomed to. Of course, she remembered this hallway from when she was a child, but amazingly, it seemed as if nothing had changed. The wallpaper still had the same garish, floral pattern on it, the cabinet with the dirty mirror still looked as antiquated as ever, and the carpet looked so old it had literally worn out in some places, only very thin strands of fibres covering up the floorboards beneath it. It was clear that this property needed redecorating, but it was also clear that Barbara had no desire or willpower to do it for the rest of the time she had left here.

Nicola felt like she would prefer to keep the front door open behind her before she went deeper into the home, as if it was some kind of mental crutch to know that she couldn't be locked in here if she closed it.

But the snow was blowing in through the doorway and reducing the temperature in this freezing home even further, so she made the decision to shut the door, even if she didn't like hearing the lock click when she did.

With the door closed, Nicola could really get a true sense of how silent the house she was standing in was. But as she listened, she heard something familiar.

She heard the ticking of the grandfather clock in the living room.

Even though she knew which way it was to get to the kitchen, Nicola felt like she wanted to peep into the other rooms while she was here, so she opened the door that led into the living room first. Just like the hallway, this room looked like it belonged in another time, and as Nicola's eyes moved from the ticking clock against the wall by the fireplace to the two armchairs that stood in front of the archaic television set, she felt another chill run through her body. But this chill had nothing to do with the weather or the fact she was in a house she hated being in. It was because seeing the two armchairs again, positioned as they were so close to each other, only reminded her of the two people who used to sit in them when she was here as a child.

Bill would sit in the left one while Barbara always occupied the one on the right, and even though Bill was gone now, Nicola could still see evidence that Barbara had continued to adhere to that tradition. That was because the tray table that Barbara presumably ate her meals at was positioned in front of the armchair on the right, suggesting that the old lady still sat in her seat and left her husband's seat vacant beside her. If she didn't know the homeowners as well as she did, then Nicola might have thought that was sweet. But knowing what she did, it only made her scoff and hate the couple even more.

There was nothing romantic about this tradition.

And there was nothing sweet about this couple.

Leaving the living room behind, Nicola moved on into the dining room, and after turning the light on, she was able to see the table and chair set in the centre of this small room, as well as the glass cupboard full of old plates and cutlery behind it. The fact that there were a couple of spider webs trailing between some of the chairs, along with the thick coating of dust on the cupboard, told Nicola that Barbara mustn't use this room very often now that she was on her own. Unlike the dining room table next door that was surrounded by warm bodies who chatted and laughed, this table lay dormant, and there was nothing about this room that suggested this was a place anybody would want to come here for dinner anytime soon.

Walking away from the depressing dining room, Nicola finally reached the kitchen, and that was where she located the fridge where she expected to find the dessert that Barbara had prepared for today. Sure enough, it was there, sitting in a large tray covered in tinfoil on the second shelf of the fridge that looked like it was straight out of an appliances catalogue from the post-war era.

Removing the tinfoil-covered tray, Nicola noticed that there wasn't much else in the way of food in this fridge. Just a bottle of milk, a tub of butter, and some yoghurt cartons. It was hardly the stuff that went into making a hearty meal, and Nicola wondered how Barbara survived on such little sustenance. Maybe she had lost her appetite since the death of her life-long partner, or perhaps she just didn't see the point in cooking much of a meal when she would be the only one eating it. Either way, it was another grim example of the kind of life Barbara had in this house while the rest of the world carried on outside without her.

As she closed the fridge, Nicola felt some satisfaction in seeing the living conditions that her elderly neighbour now resided in. Between the ancient decor, the cobwebbed-covered dining table, and the bare-bones fridge, as well as the tray table in front of the only armchair that ever got sat in these days, it appeared that Barbara was just existing now rather than really living. *There was no way the old woman could be happy here anymore by herself, was there?* Nicola wondered to herself as she prepared to leave the kitchen with the cake in her possession. But that was not her problem. As far as Nicola was concerned, the unhappier Barbara was, the better.

Passing through the hallway on the way back to the front door, Nicola felt like this visit to her neighbour's home hadn't been quite as bad as she had thought it would. Yes, it was uncomfortable for her to be back here, but the fact the property was empty made it much less troubling. It was just a very old house in very bad need of an interior designer. That was it. Nothing more. Nothing that could hurt her now.

Then she heard the creak of the floorboard above her head.

Pausing by the front door and remaining as still as she could, Nicola listened out for any further noises from upstairs. But there were none, and she figured it was nothing more than the house shifting and creaking, like buildings can even when nobody is in them. But the unexpected sound caused her to look towards the staircase, and when she did, she wondered if the upper half of the house was exactly as she remembered it, just like the lower half was.

Internally debating whether to do a little more snooping around or just return home as quickly as she could with the cake, Nicola decided that her sense of curiosity was stronger than her desire for any more food right now, so she put the cake down on the hallway cabinet and moved towards the staircase.

Putting her left foot on the bottom step, she heard the creaking sound that suggested this staircase was just one more thing in this place that needed remodelling. But she wasn't scared, at least not of any loud noises anyway.

She could never be as scared as when she was a child.

Walking up the staircase slowly and deliberately, Nicola felt that each step she took was proof of how far she had come in her life. She felt that way because there would have been a time when Nicola would never have set foot in this house again, not even for all the money in the world. But now here she was walking around this property as if she owned the place, sticking her head into rooms and enjoying the sense of freedom that came with knowing that nobody could stop her. Her confidence to not only be here but stay here for longer than she needed to was proof that she had overcome a few of her demons and was now strong enough to overcome a few more.

And there was no denying that one of those demons to overcome had a lot to do with the upper part of this house.

As she climbed towards the last step at the top of the staircase, Nicola felt herself slowing down, perhaps a sign that her brain was reminding her body that going up here might not be the best idea. But she forced herself to keep going regardless, knowing that this would be the only chance she ever got to do this and that if she could, she would fly back to Australia even more determined to keep growing as an individual and one day be a well-rounded, healthy adult who wasn't forced to live her life based on things that had happened to her in the past.

Reaching the top of the stairs, Nicola paused and looked down the dark hallway, seeing the four familiar doors that she had been expecting to see up here. She knew that the first door led into Barbara's bedroom because that had been the room she had never been allowed to go into when she was here as a child. But she wasn't interested in going in there now either, even though she could get away with it if she did, so she stopped paying attention to that door and looked across at the second one.

She knew that this particular door was the gateway into the bathroom, but having no real desire to see what was most likely a grubby bathtub and a wall of cracked tiling, she looked on again.

The third door right next to the bathroom was where Tony's bedroom had been located, and as she stood there at the top of the staircase, Nicola remembered going into that room once during her visits here. It had been a rare occasion, but she had sat on that bedroom floor and played with Tony's toys, or at least she had tried to. But it hadn't been a particularly enjoyable occasion because Nicola had known that she shouldn't have been in that room and was only going to get in trouble when she was inevitably caught there. But even then, it had been much more enjoyable than when she had been made to spend time behind the fourth and final door up here.

It was that door that was directly opposite Nicola as she continued to linger at the top of the stairs, and it was that door that she was staring at now. Behind that door was the playroom, or at least it used to be anyway. Nicola wondered if the homeowners had found a new purpose for the room once their son had grown up, but it was doubtful, considering that the rest of the house seemed to have been left exactly as it had been all those years ago. There was also a good chance it was still a playroom because Nicola knew that due to Tony's learning disabilities and overall state of mind, even though he was the same age as her now, he had retained some of those childlike qualities. It had been many years since she had seen Tony, and she had relied on her parents to update her on how the man was doing, but by all accounts, he was just a bigger, stronger version of the young boy he used to be. Conversation was difficult with him, as it had been all those years ago, and even now, he was apparently much more comfortable playing with a toy rather than doing something that would have been considered more suitable for an adult. But regardless of whether or not the fourth room up here was still a playroom, Nicola knew one thing for sure.

It was this room that she would see in her nightmares.

It would have been easy at that point to just turn around and rush back down the stairs before picking up the cake again and then leaving through the front door, slamming it shut behind her and not giving this place another second of her time. But Nicola had learnt through years of experience and heartache that often, the easiest option was not the best. Growth only came from trying to do what was hard and putting oneself in uncomfortable situations, so with that in mind, Nicola decided not to take a backwards step.

She went forward instead, towards the door at the end of the hallway.

Creeping through the hallway and hearing the floorboards groaning beneath her feet, Nicola willed herself on to keep going, desperate to prove to herself that she could do this and in the belief that when she did, she would somehow be stronger for the experience. But then she reached the door, and all that determination and self-belief went away, replaced instead by the same emotions that had often got the better of her in the past.

Standing there with her fingers on the door handle, it took her no time at all to feel weak, hopeless, and scared all over again. It also took her no time to turn and rush back along the hallway and down the stairs, almost tripping and missing a couple of steps as she left in such haste.

Grabbing the cake as her eyes were flooded with tears, Nicola only started to feel a little bit better once she had opened the front door and stepped outside into the snow again.

The frigid air stung the wet parts of her face where her tears had streamed down from her eyes, and she almost fell again as she rushed through the snow without regard for what obstacles might have been beneath it. But none of that mattered right now.

All that mattered was that she was out of that house again.

10

Nicola was cold, wet, and out of breath by the time she got back into her parents' house, but one thing she had stopped being was upset. That was because she had paused on the driveway and wiped away her tears to make sure that Barbara would have no idea of the emotions that had been stirred up inside of her when she re-entered the house.

It was important for Nicola not to show any weakness in front of the older woman, and so far, she seemed to have managed that. But going next door had easily been her biggest test of the day, even more so than sitting across the table from her elderly neighbour, and that was why she had lingered outside for a little longer to ensure that her eyes were dry and her heart rate had come back down to a more manageable level.

'There you are!' John cried when he saw his daughter coming through the front door. 'We were starting to wonder where you had got to.'

'The snow is really bad,' Nicola replied, hoping her excuse of the extreme weather would prevent him from asking any more questions about why she had taken so long getting the cake.

'Thanks for doing that, love,' John said as he took the cake from her. 'It would have been bad to send Barbara outside.'

Nicola didn't say anything to that, choosing silence over saying that she wished that old woman had to spend the night out in that snow because she would surely freeze to death, and then there would finally be some new neighbours next door.

After taking off her coat and getting another glass of wine from the kitchen, Nicola reluctantly returned to the dining room to see that Barbara was still sitting at the table and still chatting away with the rest of her family members.

As Ruth and John got the desserts ready for serving in the kitchen, Nicola re-took her seat at the table just in time to hear her brother finish telling Barbara the story of how he had met his wife.

'That's wonderful,' Barbara said, clapping her hands together and seemingly feeling overjoyed at what she had just heard, which was possibly genuine but most likely more acting on the part of the deceptive old lady. 'Very original. I haven't heard of any other couples meeting in that fashion.'

'Yeah, I guess it makes for a good story if nothing else,' Charlotte said as she smiled at her husband, and Nicola knew it was a good story because she had heard it back when she had first found out that her brother was getting serious with her now sister-in-law.

But she was glad she hadn't had to sit through it again, just like she was glad when her parents appeared with the desserts because the sight of the last course of the meal meant that it wouldn't be too long now until everybody got to leave this dinner table and when they did, Nicola hoped that would be the time when Barbara left this house.

As Ruth and John put down the plates that contained the options for dessert, everyone around the table eyed the cakes and pudding eagerly, although there was one problem that Nicola had spotted. One of the options was a lemon cheesecake, and that was an issue because she couldn't eat lemon. She was allergic to it, so why had her mother made such a cake for Christmas dinner? But then she realised who had actually made it.

This was the cake Barbara had 'kindly' contributed.

'Here, let me cut you all a piece,' Barbara said as she carefully picked up the big knife in the middle of the table and used the blade to slice into the lemon cake.

‘This looks lovely,’ Ruth said, and her husband agreed as he accepted his slice of the cake. ‘But you really shouldn’t have gone to the trouble.’

‘It was no trouble,’ Barbara replied as she cut a second piece and gave it to Ruth. ‘I always liked baking for Bill, but I haven’t done much of it since he passed. It was nice to get my apron on again and prove to myself that I could still do it.’

‘Well, you certainly can,’ Ruth said as she joined her husband in tucking into the cake with her fork.

Barbara smiled as she cut a very large slice of cake for Colin before going to cut another one for Charlotte.

‘Oh, not for me, thank you, Barbara,’ Charlotte suddenly said. ‘I’m trying to be good, so I’m only going to allow myself one cake, and I think I’d like a piece of the pudding if that’s okay.’

There didn’t seem to be anything wrong with Charlotte’s polite refusal of the lemon cake, but Barbara simply shook her head and smiled before cutting the slice anyway and putting it onto a plate.

‘Don’t be silly, my dear,’ Barbara said as she placed the plate down in front of Charlotte. ‘Christmas day is no time to try and be good. Santa has already been, after all. Now it’s time to be a little sinful.’

With that, she gave Charlotte a wink, and Nicola watched as her sister-in-law could not help but give in to the older woman’s reasoning.

‘Okay, Nicola, your turn,’ Barbara said as she went to cut another slice, but it was at that point that

Ruth stopped her and rather awkwardly had to remind the cake-cutter that Nicola could not eat lemon.

'Oh my gosh, I'm so sorry,' Barbara said, looking at Nicola mortified. 'Of course, I remember now. I can't believe I forgot. Forgive me. I would have made something else if I'd have remembered.'

Nicola said nothing as she stared at the yellow cake on the table in front of her, before shrugging and instead turning her attention to the Christmas pudding beside it. But it wasn't that she was frustrated or upset about not being able to partake in the lemon cake consumption today. It was because Nicola knew there was no way Barbara would have forgotten about her allergy, so that meant she had obviously done it on purpose. It was most likely just a discreet way of the old woman being mean to Nicola, but even so, it was nowhere near on the level of what had happened in the past, so the younger woman wasn't going to worry too much about this one.

'Okay, Ben, you're up,' Barbara said as she cut a small piece of cake but again, she had to stop when Charlotte told her that her son did not like lemon cake, and he was happy with the chocolate cake that he was already tucking into.

'No problem,' Barbara said as she put down the knife, and with everybody seemingly taken care of, she smiled before turning her attention to the Christmas pudding.

'I think I might try some of this if you don't mind,' she said, and Ruth told her that was fine before instructing John to cut their neighbour a piece himself.

'Don't you want some of your lemon cake before it's all gone?' Charlotte asked Barbara, but she just simply smiled and shook her head. 'I must confess to something terrible. I actually made two lemon cakes the other day and ended up eating most of the other one myself, so I think I've had my fill of that particular dessert.'

Everybody laughed at her admission, except Nicola who just let out a sigh and wished again for this excruciating dinner to be over. She couldn't believe that she had come all the way back from Australia for Christmas only to end up having to sit with and listen to Barbara, a woman she despised, making jokes at her dinner table. All she could hope for now was that Barbara would be tired after the meal was finished, and she might retire early back to her own home, leaving Nicola to enjoy what was left of Christmas Day in peace with her family.

But that remained to be seen.

Ten minutes later, it was clear that Barbara's lemon cake had proved to be very popular because all that remained on the tray were a few yellow crumbs, and Nicola's family members sat back with their hands on their stomachs and smiles on their faces as they complimented the baker on her tasty treat.

Barbara seemed thrilled about the fact that her contribution to this meal had been a roaring success, and it was just one more thing for Nicola to feel agitated about as she impatiently drummed her fingers on the table and checked the time.

‘Have you got somewhere to be?’ her dad asked her when he noticed her watching the clock.

‘Oh, no,’ she replied with a shrug. ‘Just seeing what time it is.’

‘I think it’s time to go on a diet,’ Charlotte quipped, jesting about how much everybody around this table had consumed today, and everybody laughed before realising the best way to forget about all those extra calories was to dispose of the evidence as quickly as possible.

With the table being cleared and the meal drawing to a close, Nicola seized her opportunity to get out of the dining room, and she asked Ben if he would like to go and play with some of his new toys in the living room. The young boy happily agreed to that idea, and Nicola felt a sense of relief as she left Barbara behind and took her nephew into another room. With a bit of luck, she hoped Barbara would be saying her goodbyes soon, and Nicola might not have to put up with her for much longer. But ten minutes later and Barbara was sat on one of the sofas with a cup of tea in her hand and seemingly in no rush to leave this house and go back to her own. Instead, she was happily chatting away with Colin and Charlotte while also watching Ben playing with Nicola.

Nicola had the sinking feeling that Barbara was going to hang around all day, and if so, Christmas was definitely ruined this year. But what could she do? It would hardly look well for her to tell Barbara to put her coat on and get out. But as she lay there on the carpet beside her nephew and helped him construct some kind of battlefield for his soldiers, she made a decision.

Either her family came to her in Australia at Christmas now, or Nicola would stay away from home.

She would stay away until she heard that Barbara had died.

Nicola's sense of hatred for the elderly woman was so strong that she didn't even feel an ounce of guilt for thinking in that way. She was simply being honest with herself. She no longer wished to travel halfway around the world to spend time with her loved ones if it meant that time could be ruined by the presence of Barbara. Not only was it a waste of time and money, but it was only reminding Nicola of how powerless she had used to feel, and one of the main reasons she had moved so far away from home was to forget about that feeling as much as possible. But right here, it was being rammed down her throat almost as much as her family members had rammed the neighbour's lemon cake into their mouths at the dinner table.

With the dishwasher loaded and turned on and the kitchen returned to some kind of order, John and Ruth joined everybody else in the living room to settle down and see what was on TV. Being Christmas Day, there was plenty of choice, and it didn't take long for everyone to agree on a festive film to watch to while away the next couple of hours or so. At this point, Nicola was wishing away the whole day, and she couldn't wait to get in bed tonight because that would mean this charade was over for her. But it was about halfway into the movie when she started getting the first impressions that this day might only just be beginning.

The room had gone very quiet, barring the noise from the TV, of course, and when Nicola had looked around, she had noticed that several of her family members had their eyes closed and had seemingly fallen asleep. It was only Ben who was still awake, playing with his toys while Barbara sipped her tea and enjoyed the movie. But everyone else was asleep.

Checking the time, Nicola saw that it was by no means late, so she couldn't believe that her parents, her brother, and her sister-in-law had dozed off. Sure, they had all eaten a lot of food and were feeling a little sleepy, but what were the chances of them all drifting off into a slumber at the same time? That was why she decided to try and wake them.

Reaching over to her brother first, Nicola shook his arm to try and wake him. But he didn't respond, nor did he open his eyes when his sister called his name. Trying Charlotte, Nicola got the same response, and that was when she really started to get concerned. Ben had noticed too, and he wanted to know why everyone was sleeping.

Attempting to wake up her parents next, Nicola again failed to get a response out of them, and that was when she knew something was wrong. It was at that point that Ben started to become upset, and he wanted to know what was wrong with his family members, but he wasn't the only one. Nicola wanted to know too, and that was when she saw Barbara still sitting on the sofa and sipping her cup of tea with a knowing smile on her face.

‘What’s happened to them?’ Nicola cried when she realised the old woman might have caused this.

But Barbara didn’t answer. She just looked at the four ‘sleeping’ adults and smiled again.

Were they unconscious?

Or they were dead?

‘Mummy! Daddy!’ Ben cried as he tried to wake up his sleeping parents, and Nicola was just as desperate as she tried to get a response out of her parents, but not a single one of the four family members gave any indication that they were waking back up.

Realising this was bad, Nicola scrambled in her pocket for her mobile phone, desperately trying to call for an ambulance as quickly as possible before any more time was lost. But as she started to dial, she heard Barbara’s voice behind her.

‘I guess they really did like my lemon cake,’ she said.

Nicola froze when she realised what the woman was hinting at.

Had the cake been spiked? Had their neighbour poisoned them?

If so, why?

But Nicola knew the most important thing to do first was to call the emergency services. There would be time to deal with Barbara after that. Right now, the priority had to be saving her family.

As Nicola pressed the three 9’s on her phone that would connect her to the operator who could send an ambulance to this house as quickly as possible, she failed to notice that somebody else had entered the room behind her. It was actually Ben who noticed first, and he pointed towards the door over Nicola's left shoulder to let her know that someone else was here.

But she didn't get a chance to turn around.

Instead, everything suddenly went black.

11

The first thing Nicola noticed when she opened her eyes was that she had the world's worst headache. But the second thing she noticed was that she couldn't put her hands to her head to check on what might be causing her pain because they were bound by duct tape, tied behind her back and fastened around the chair she was sitting on.

Realising that she was restrained, Nicola began to panic and tried to call out for help, but her voice was nothing but a dry croak, hinting that it might have been a while since she lubricated her throat. Her dehydration and headache were no doubt made worse by all of the wine she had consumed during Christmas dinner, but that felt like a long time ago now.

But was that the case? What time was it?

And where the hell was she?

Looking around, Nicola saw a bare brick wall to her left and a generic plasterboard wall straight ahead. There was another brick wall on her right, and as she started to panic a little more that she was really trapped in some kind of tomb, she strained against her restraints to turn her head and see over her shoulder to check out what was behind her. But when she managed it, she saw that there was a door in this room, and it was about twenty feet away.

That meant that there was a way out.

She just had to get to it.

Attempting to get to her feet, Nicola was then met with the grim realisation that it wasn't just her hands that were tied together. Her feet were too, her ankles wrapped together in thick tape, and while they weren't fastened to the chair like her hands were, it was clear she was going to have a very hard time moving around. But that couldn't stop her, not if she wanted to get out of here and not if she wanted to save her family.

What had happened to them? They had been poisoned, Nicola remembered. But why? And where was Ben now? Was he safe?

Nicola struggled to keep herself calm as she realised she had absolutely no idea what the answers were to any of those questions, just like she had no idea how she had ended up in this room. Had she been hit over the head? That would explain why her skull was throbbing, as well as why she didn't recall being put in this room and tied to this chair. But regardless of how, why, and what had happened, Nicola knew only one thing mattered now. She had to get out of here and try and find her family, so that meant she was going to have to get to that door, regardless of how crippled she was by her restraints.

Opting to try shuffling first, Nicola wriggled her body in the hope that it would be enough to move the chair and get her closer towards the door behind her. But that didn't work, and while the chair creaked and groaned beneath her, it barely moved, meaning she was just as far away as before she had started expending all that energy.

Trying to think straight with her head still feeling like it was going to explode was difficult, but Nicola had to focus and try and figure a way out of here. She couldn't get off this chair, which meant she was having a hard time moving. Therefore, there was only one thing for it.

Taking a deep breath, Nicola started to wriggle again in her seat before she built up enough momentum to be able to rock the chair from side to side, tipping it on both of its left legs and then its right. The more she forced it, the more severe the tipping angle became, but that was what she wanted, and as she kept going, it was inevitable that gravity would eventually take over and cause the chair to topple to one side or the other. In the end, it fell to the left, and as it did, Nicola heard the chair crack as it hit the ground before she felt her arms becoming a little freer than they had felt before. They were still tied behind her back, but they were no longer entangled in the chair, and now she was able to be a little more mobile, she knew she could begin the tedious process of trying to shuffle and crawl her way over to the door.

Nicola groaned and gasped as she tried her hardest to move herself across the harsh, concrete floor in this prison she found herself in, and while the surface was not kind to her body, she was slowly but surely getting closer to the door. The only problem was the arduous task was depleting her of what little energy she felt she had, but that was the price to pay if she wanted to get out of here, and she most certainly wanted to do that.

She wanted to check if her family was okay. She wanted to find out how and why all this craziness had happened. And most of all, she wanted to make Barbara pay because whatever was going on here, that old woman was definitely behind it.

Having made it away from the broken chair and halfway to the door, Nicola paused for a moment to get her breath back and give her aching body a short reprieve from being hauled across the concrete before she resumed her escape attempt. It was tough, but the pain and fatigue she felt was no match for the anger and determination bubbling away inside of her, and that was why she eventually made it to where she wanted to be.

Nicola was at the foot of the door.

Now all she had to do was try and open it.

Looking up at the handle above her head, Nicola wondered how she was supposed to pull on it with her hands tied behind her back. Then she figured that she might be able to do it if she could get to her feet and stand with her back towards the door, so her next task was to try and get herself upright.

Pressing herself against the doorframe, Nicola strained every sinew in her body as she forced herself against the door and dug her heels into the ground, looking to gain as much momentum as she could that would move her upwards now. But it was even harder to do this than it had been to crawl across the concrete floor with her hands and legs tied, and despite her best efforts, she just couldn't manage to stand up.

'Damn it!' she cried after another exhausting attempt had failed, and she felt tears of frustration filling her eyes before she clenched her teeth and vowed to try again because failure was not an option here.

Letting out a cry of desperation as she made another attempt, Nicola used nothing but sheer will to get herself up, and as she made it to her feet, she almost laughed because it felt as if she had overcome odds that had been so far stacked against her that she should never have made it this far. But now she had, all she had to do was get her hands on that door handle, and then she would be out of here.

Feeling around behind her back, Nicola was able to locate the handle before getting her body into a position where she would be able to get some purchase on it and actually move it down so it would open. But even though she managed to do that, it turned out to be a complete waste of time.

The door was locked.

Of course it was.

'No!' Nicola cried, this time finding it much harder to control her emotions because now it felt like she had run out of options. If this door wouldn't open then she couldn't escape, and what did that mean for her and the rest of her family?

Realising that this door was the difference between what felt like life or death, Nicola slammed her shoulder into it as hard as she could. She did it again and again, ignoring the growing pain in her bones as she continued to try and force it to open with her bodyweight. But it wouldn't budge, and after several long and draining minutes, Nicola was done.

That was when she slid back down to the ground and sat there, the tears in her eyes flowing freely now and her heart hammering so hard in her chest that she felt it might burst through.

Then she heard the sound of a key turning in a lock.

Looking at the door, Nicola saw the handle moving, and she wished she was still on her feet so she could rush towards the gap that was surely about to be created in the doorway. But she was on the ground, and she already knew it was no easy feat to get back up, not that she wouldn't try. But no sooner had she thought about getting up again then she saw the door open, and she saw who it was on the other side of it.

It was Barbara. And the old lady seemed happy about something.

'Is that you making all that noise?' she asked Nicola as she stood over her and grinned. 'Wow, I see that you have been busy. It looks like you've broken one of my chairs.'

Barbara's eyes moved from Nicola to the damaged chair behind her and then back again to the woman by her feet.

'What are you doing?' Nicola cried, desperate for answers. 'What have you done to my family?'

'Calm down, dear. You're going to strain your voice with all that shouting.'

'Tell me what you've done!'

Nicola tried to move towards Barbara, but it was easy for the older woman to step back and get away from her. After all, Nicola couldn't grab or kick. Her limbs were still restrained, and because of that, Barbara was not at all worried.

'I'll tell you all about my plans in good time,' she said to Nicola once the woman on the floor had calmed down a little bit. 'But first, I want you to relax and enjoy being back in my home again.'

'What are you talking about?' Nicola cried as she looked around her because she did not recognise this room as being a part of her neighbour's home.

'What's the matter? Don't you recognise this place?' Barbara said before tutting and seemingly remembering something. 'Oh, that's right. I don't think this was one of the rooms you ever went in when we used to babysit for you. You're in the basement.'

Nicola tried to process what she was being told, but no matter how hard she tried, it didn't make sense or sound good. Why the hell was she in the basement?

'I don't think your mum and dad have utilised the space under their home, but Bill and I did. We've had this basement for a long time, but he used to come down here a lot more than I did. I never cared for this place that much. But now I see that it has its uses.'

'What do you want?' Nicola cried. 'Why are you doing this?'

'That's no way to talk to your babysitter,' Barbara said as her expression and tone of voice suddenly got much darker. 'You used to be a lot politer than that.'

'What are you talking about? You're not my babysitter!' Nicola cried, exasperated because none of this was making any sense to her.

But then Barbara leaned down and looked the younger woman in the eyes before smiling again and patting her on the head as if she really was a child.

'Maybe not anymore,' Barbara said so calmly that it sent a chill down Nicola's spine. 'But I used to be. And we both know that I still have all the power between us, don't we?'

With that, she turned and left the room, closing and locking the door behind herself and leaving Nicola shouting out for the old woman to come back. But she didn't.

She left Nicola in the basement.

She left her alone to try and figure out what was going on by herself.

12

1990

'But I don't want to go to their house!'

Nicola stomped her feet and clenched her fists and those actions, along with her desperate cry of determination, highlighted how much of a small ball of fury she was right now. She might have only been six, but she had no problem letting her feelings be known to those who were older than her. That was why her parents were finding her much harder to raise than they had her brother, who was eight, and had been no trouble so far.

'It's just for a couple of hours,' Ruth told her daughter as she continued to pack her son's swimming bag for the race he was taking part in at the local leisure centre this afternoon. 'Then we'll be round to pick you up.'

'No, I'm not going!' Nicola replied, just as adamant as she had been the first time her mother had told her about the plan to leave her with their next-door neighbours while they took Colin swimming.

'Well, you can't stay here on your own, can you?' Ruth said as she felt herself becoming more exasperated with every minute that passed by on what was proving to be another tiring weekend of looking after her two children until school resumed again on Monday. 'And we're not taking you with us again because you did nothing but complain last time and ruin it for all the other families who were trying to watch the swimming.'

'Mum!' Nicola moaned, her limited vocabulary meaning she was struggling to find more words to argue her point. 'I'm not going. It'll be boooorrring!'

'You can take some of your dolls. And I'm sure they'll let you watch TV.'

'I don't want to go! I want to stay here!'

'No, it's been decided. Bill and Barbara have kindly offered to look after you for us, and we're dropping you off next door. That's it. End of discussion.'

To prove that last statement, Ruth zipped up the bag she had just packed for her son and picked it up before heading for the door. She had gone back to packing Colin's swimwear ever since he had turned up at the last race without his trunks and towel, and it was just a little more evidence that both of her children had a lot more growing up to do yet.

'No! You can't make me!' Nicola cried, and Ruth turned around in the doorway to see her daughter with her arms crossed and her bottom lip down, which was presumably supposed to make her look defiant but only made her look quite comical in the end.

'Do you want me to tell your father that you're being trouble for me?' she asked the stroppy six-year-old in the bedroom, turning to a tactic that had worked quite well in the past. It was the tactic of inducing fear in the child because if John got involved in a dispute, it usually meant things were even less likely to go well for Nicola.

'No!' she replied rather wisely, aware that she was no match for her dad in the arguing stakes.

'Okay then. Get your shoes on, and get ready to go because we're leaving in five minutes.'

With that, Ruth left the room and left Nicola with little option but to do as her mother had told her.

Stomping all the way out of her parents' bedroom and into her own, Nicola continued to huff and puff as she picked out the dolls she felt like she wanted to take next door. She still didn't want to have to go to her neighbours' house, but it seemed like she had no choice, so she might as well try and take as much as she could with her.

Filling her school rucksack with as many dolls as she could cram in, Nicola heard her mother calling her from downstairs and knew she was out of time. With another deep sigh, the young girl reluctantly left her bedroom and made her way downstairs, making sure to stamp her feet loudly on each step as she went to prove to everybody in this house that she was still not happy about her situation. Not that it seemed to do her much good or even gain her much attention. Neither one of her parents said anything as they put on their own coats and shoes, while her brother just stood by with his swimming bag slung over his shoulder and that gormless look on his face that he usually displayed.

Nicola put her own shoes on and was just about ready to go when her dad noticed the bag on her shoulders and asked her what was in there.

'My dolls,' she told him. 'Mummy said I could take some.'

'Yeah, you can take some. Not all of them. How many have you got in there?' John asked as he tried to feel the weight of the bag, and despite being much bigger and stronger than his daughter, he was still surprised by the volume of it.

'I want to take these,' Nicola told him, suddenly afraid that she was going to be made to put back some of her dolls, and that would have made this situation even worse for her. But one silver lining of this whole thing seemed to be that the family had now run out of time and had to leave immediately if they were going to make it to the leisure centre in time for the start of Colin's race.

Trudging out of the house with a backpack full of dolls, Nicola looked towards the house next door, where she knew she would be spending the next couple of hours. That amount of time felt like an eternity to her, as it usually did for most children with a loose concept of time, and she already couldn't wait for when she was able to be back home again.

As John and Colin got into the family car, Ruth walked with Nicola to the next house and knocked on the front door.

'Why couldn't they look after me at our house?' Nicola wanted to know, curious as to why Bill and Barbara hadn't just come to them.

'Because they're doing us the favour, so they get to stay at their house if they want to,' Ruth replied before the door in front of them was unlocked and pulled open to reveal one of the homeowners on the other side.

It was Bill, and the forty-two-year-old man smiled when he saw the mother and daughter standing on his doorstep.

'Hi, guys!'

‘Hi, Bill. Am I okay to drop Nicola off? We’re leaving now.’

‘Yes, that’s absolutely fine. No problem at all. Come in.’

Bill stepped aside to allow the child to enter, but she instinctively lingered beside her mother rather than enter the unfamiliar home with the unfamiliar man.

It wasn’t unusual for any six-year-old to be shy around a stranger, and Nicola was no different, but as much as Ruth sympathised with her child’s nervousness, she didn’t have time to spend too long easing her into her new surroundings.

‘It’s just for a couple of hours,’ she reminded Nicola. ‘I’ll be back to get you then, okay?’

Nicola nodded her head slowly, but she was still unsure about all of this, which Bill picked up on as he tried to make those next two hours seem a little more appealing to her.

‘We’ve got lots for you to do here,’ he told the unsure girl. ‘You can help Barbara with some baking, or you can play in the playroom if you’d like.’

Nicola’s ears pricked up at the mention of a playroom, and suddenly, this didn’t seem like the worst thing in the world.

‘I’ve brought my dolls,’ she told Bill to make sure that he knew she already had in mind what she wanted to spend her time playing with.

‘That’s great!’ Bill replied enthusiastically, and he stepped aside a little more to make the gap in the doorway even bigger for Nicola to walk through.

Glancing up at her mother one more time for confirmation that everything was okay and she should just go ahead and enter the house, Ruth smiled at her daughter and gave her a gentle nudge in the direction of the door. With that, Nicola entered her neighbour's home.

'Make sure you behave!' Ruth warned her daughter before Bill could say goodbye and close the door, and Nicola nodded her head. 'And just a reminder she has a lemon allergy,' Ruth told Bill, and he assured her that he remembered that from one of their previous conversations.

With that, the goodbyes were said and the door was closed, and Nicola found herself feeling a little lonely as she looked around at the décor that differed greatly to how her own home looked.

'Barbara! The girl's here!' Bill called out before walking away into one of the rooms, and Nicola wondered what she was supposed to do as she remained standing by the door, unsure about if she should follow the man or wait to be told what to do.

The house seemed very quiet, barring the sound of a ticking clock, and Nicola wondered if anybody else was in, or at least she did until she heard footsteps on the staircase and looked up to see Barbara descending towards her.

'Hello, dear,' she said with a warm smile. 'What have you got in your bag?'

'My dolls,' Nicola replied meekly.

'How wonderful. Do you want to show me?'

Nicola nodded her head as she heard the television go on in the room that Bill had just disappeared into.

'Come on. Let's go into the kitchen, and you can show me. I'm just finishing baking a cake. Do you like cake?'

There weren't many children that would have answered that question negatively, and after confirming that she did like cake, Barbara told Nicola that there was a piece for her just as soon as it was ready.

As she took a seat at the kitchen table and started to take out her dolls, Nicola wondered where Tony, the six-year-old who lived here, was and, more specifically, where the playroom was. But she soon stopped thinking about those things when she saw Barbara open the oven and remove the tray on which there was a very big sponge cake.

Barbara whistled as she worked, setting the cake down before turning off the oven and going into the cutlery drawer from which she took out a big knife and placed it down beside the dessert she had just made. Nicola found herself watching the woman, intrigued as she observed the grown-up performing adult tasks, mainly because being that age seemed so far away from her own. Nicola often liked to play with her dolls and their dollhouses and pretend like she had her own house where she could cook and clean and be in charge of things. But that was a long way off yet, as she was often reminded of by her parents, who always treated her like such a child. But so far, Barbara or Bill hadn't treated Nicola like a child. They were just going about their business in a very calm fashion, and it was having an almost soothing effect on the young girl at the table.

'We'll have to let the cake cool down a little before we eat it,' Barbara advised, and Nicola nodded her head to show that she understood before the older woman came and took a seat beside her at the table.

'Now then, what do we have here?' she asked as she looked around at the dolls that Nicola had removed from her bag.

'These are my dolls,' Nicola replied matter-of-factly, and Barbara smiled at that example of stating the obvious before pointing to the one in the white dress.

'Who is this one?'

'That's Lucy.'

'Well, hello Lucy. I like your dress.'

Nicola smiled because she liked Lucy's dress too.

'Who's this?' Barbara asked, moving on to the doll with the red hat.

'That's Rebecca. She's new.'

'Yes, she certainly looks new. And she looks very pretty in her hat. May I?'

Barbara checked with Nicola before picking up the doll for a closer look, and the young girl hesitated for a moment before nodding to show that it would be fine.

'She really is pretty,' Barbara said as she examined the doll. 'When did you get her?'

'Last Christmas.'

'Wow, you must have been a good girl if Santa brought you a present like this.'

Nicola nodded her head, still feeling a little unsure about her environment and the people in this house but warming to it all a little more by the minute. Her dolls were her favourite topic of conversation, and that sponge cake sitting on the kitchen counter certainly did look and smell good.

'Are you always a good girl for your mummy and daddy?' Barbara asked as she put the doll in the hat down and looked back at Nicola.

'Most of the time,' Nicola replied, humorous in her honesty, and Barbara smiled.

'That's good. Children should be well behaved.'

It was at that point that Nicola again wondered where Barbara and Bill's son was, and she looked towards the door to see if there was any sign of him coming to see her.

'Tony is here,' Barbara said at that moment as if reading the little girl's mind. 'He's upstairs in his bedroom. But he won't be coming out to play today.'

'Why not?'

'Because unlike you, he has not been well behaved.'

'What did he do?'

'That's not the point. The point is that he knows he was naughty, and he knows he is not allowed to be like that. So that's why he won't be playing with any toys today, nor will he be getting any cake because cake is for good children. Children like you.'

Barbara smiled at Nicola again, and while the girl was still wondering about Tony and what he could have done to get into trouble, she did like the fact that she was still going to be allowed some cake today.

'I think it should have cooled down by now,' Barbara said, looking over at the cake sitting on the counter. 'What do you think? Is it ready for us to try a piece?'

Nicola nodded her head eagerly, desperate for that piece to be on her plate in front of her as soon as possible. But before Barbara got up and went to cut into the cake, she suddenly leaned in closer to Nicola and lowered her voice.

'Can you keep a secret?' she asked the child beside her.

Nicola was suddenly unsure and wondered if this was some kind of a test that her mum had set up for her.

'My parents have told me that I shouldn't keep secrets,' she replied, and Barbara smiled because she appreciated both the honesty from the young girl and the good intentions from her parents. But then she spoke again.

'Not all secrets are bad, though. You do know that, right?'

Nicola was unsure, so she didn't say anything, prompting Barbara to speak again.

'Some secrets are okay. Like if I was to have two pieces of cake now but didn't tell my husband, that would be our little secret, wouldn't it?'

Nicola thought about it for a moment before figuring that a secret such as that was okay.

‘Here’s another example,’ Barbara said. ‘If we were to play games with these dolls that were just between us, that would be our little secret, and that would be okay too, wouldn’t it?’

Nicola didn’t see any problem with playing games with her dolls and keeping it a secret, so she nodded her head to that one too.

‘Great,’ Barbara said, clapping her hands together before getting up from her seat. ‘We can be secret buddies. Now, what do you say to some cake?’

‘Yes, please,’ Nicola replied, and by the time she had the cake in front of her and a fork in her hand, Nicola was feeling much better about being here in this house with these people. Maybe it wouldn’t be so bad if she had to come here every now and again while her brother was swimming in races. Maybe she would enjoy herself if she just got to talk about and play with her dolls and eat cake and keep some small secrets with Barbara. Maybe this might actually end up being a lot of fun.

Or maybe she was very wrong about all of that.

13

PRESENT DAY

The fact that it wasn't pitch-black in this basement that was holding Nicola was one small slice of consolation for the trapped woman as she sat with her back to the wall and her limbs still restrained. Staring at the door that hadn't opened since Barbara had locked it behind herself earlier, Nicola stared at the small amount of light that was getting under the door because it was the only thing providing her with any comfort at this time. She was still trapped in here, she still had no idea what had happened to the rest of her family, and most of all, she had no idea how she could improve her situation anytime soon. All she could do was keep looking at that yellow glow and hoping that it never went out because it if did, it wouldn't just be the light that had been extinguished then.

It would be her last bit of hope too.

Resting her aching skull against the brick wall behind her, Nicola's eyes moved around the room and looked once more for anything that could help her get out of here. But just like all the other times she had done this exercise, all she saw was the broken chair and the walls.

The broken chair might have been useful for her if her hands had been free because she could have at least picked up one of the legs and then used it as a weapon whenever Barbara came back in here. But without the full use of her hands to swing the chair leg, she stood no chance of doing any damage to the old woman and that fact combined with her ankles being tied also meant that even if she could get past Barbara, it would take her a very long time to hop to safety.

Letting out a deep sigh, Nicola gave up on fantasising about using the chair as her means of escape and instead looked around at the only other things in this damn room.

The walls.

But there was even less hope to be garnered there because unless she had suddenly developed the ability to pass through bricks and mortar, then she wasn't going to find her escape that way either. However, with absolutely nothing else to look at, Nicola kept running her eyes across the borders that held her, and as she did, she realised that one of the walls might actually offer a glimmer of hope. That's because three of them were made from brick, but the one opposite her was built with a different material, possibly plasterboard, and Nicola wondered if it was weak enough to break through.

Going through the exhausting task of getting herself upright again, Nicola was able to get back to her feet, and after taking a few moments to steady her balance and ensure that she wasn't going to topple over without her hands being able to break her fall, she began hopping across the basement.

It took her a while because she had to keep stopping for fear of falling flat on her face, but eventually she made it all the way over to the opposing wall, and when she did, she turned and ran her hands against the surface of it.

It was smooth, not at all like the harsh brickwork that she had just been sitting against, and even better than that, it felt a little springy too. What was it? Painted plywood or plasterboard? Whatever it was, Nicola started to push against it in the hope that she could break through. But it didn't budge, as most walls tended not to do, and once again, it seemed like a lost cause. But being unprepared to be stuck down here in this gloomy dungeon for however long Barbara decided, Nicola felt like she had to try whatever she could to get out of here. That was why she lifted her arms slightly before driving her elbow into the surface of the wall as hard as she could.

She had been anticipating that it might hurt, and it did, but she had also been hoping for something too, and when she saw that it had materialised, she felt a surge of optimism pass through her. She had created a sizeable dent in the wall, and while it was hardly anything to get too excited about it yet, it did represent possibility.

The possibility that Nicola could break through here.

She had no idea what was on the other side of this wall, and for all she knew, there was just an even sturdier wall beyond it, but she had nothing else to work with, so she dug her elbow into it again. And again. And again.

Nicola elbowed the wall so many times that the body part soon went numb, but that didn't stop her because the more she worked, the bigger the hole she created. She had been right about this wall possibly being made of plasterboard because the fact it was breaking apart so easily as she struck it reminded her of the time her brother had punched a hole in the wall of his bedroom. Nicola had been ten years old when she heard her brother arguing with their parents, and after her sibling had stormed up the stairs and slammed his bedroom door, she heard a series of loud noises, most of which later turned out to be him putting his fist through the wall. That obviously led to him being grounded for several weeks as well as a redecoration project for their dad to take care of, but as well as that, it taught Nicola that some walls weren't as strong as they appeared. And this wall was just another example of that.

What had originally been a barrier was now quickly breaking down and becoming a possible way out, but only if the hole Nicola was creating actually led anywhere.

That remained to be seen, but Nicola kept on elbowing the drywall as hard as she could until her damaged limb ached, and her eyes stung with tears. Then she stopped and observed her work, and when she did, she saw that the hole was at least big enough for her to poke her head into now.

Leaning forward and peering through the gap she had created in the wall, Nicola hoped she might see something that could give her a way out. But what she saw was most unexpected. There was another room on the other side of this wall consisting of a bed, a chair, and a small dresser table, and while nobody was in there at the moment, it was obvious it had recently been used because the duvet on the mattress was turned open as if someone had climbed out from under it.

Why the hell was there a bedroom down here?

Who was sleeping in the basement?

As Nicola puzzled over it, she realised that there would be an explanation for this, just like there could be an explanation for how a seventy-three-year-old woman had been able to carry her unconscious body down to this basement in the first place. Barbara's son, Tony, must have been home for Christmas after all, and he must have carried Nicola down here. This must also be where he stayed while he was home, although why he wasn't allowed to sleep in the main house was not clear. But one thing was for sure. He was sleeping down here.

Nicola did not know what she was supposed to do with that information because as shocking as it was, all she really cared about was getting out of here. So, unless something in this hidden bedroom could help her then it wasn't very useful.

Examining the secret room again through the hole, Nicola looked for something that might help her remove her restraints and at least be able to move more freely. But as she did, she realised something else. If Tony was sleeping down here, then that meant he had to have a way in. He obviously wasn't required to smash through this temporary wall every time he wanted to go to bed, so that must mean there was a door somewhere.

And if there was a door, it might mean there was an exit.

Nicola's heart began to race as she realised she genuinely might have a chance of getting out of here. But she needed to stay calm because she hadn't yet found that way out, and wherever it was, she needed to find it before Barbara came back into the basement and saw the damaged wall.

Her first thought was to resume hitting the wall so she could eventually make the hole big enough to crawl through. She knew that would involve making more noise that could potentially be heard by Barbara, as well as ensuring her sore elbow would hurt even more, but now that she had discovered what she had, Nicola went back to work with a renewed focus and intensity.

Elbowing the edge of the hole and breaking away even more of the cheaply constructed wall, Nicola figured this partition had been put in to conceal the bedroom, which explained why it was different to the other walls in this basement and also why it was nowhere near as sturdy. She didn't know how old it was, but one thing was clear. It was becoming less of a wall by the minute and would require some serious repairing by the time Nicola was done with it.

But that was not her concern as she kept hitting the drywall and enlarging the gap, but it was as she was doing so that something rather unexpected happened.

A door opened at the far end of the wall to where she was working.

A door…

This was her way into this bedroom beyond.

Nicola stopped what she was doing and stared at the door, which had presumably opened by itself thanks to all the vibrations she was sending along the wall as she had pummelled it. The outline of the door had been so well concealed that she hadn't even noticed it was there, but she knew about it now, so she hopped towards it with hope in her heart.

If she could go into this next room, then maybe there was a way out from there. After all, who could say what other surprises were waiting for her in this basement that was becoming more unusual by the minute?

Opening the door fully and looking inside, Nicola saw the bed, the chair, and the dresser table that she had seen through the hole, but this time, she was able to get closer to them, and she passed through the doorway to get a better look.

When she did, she was able to see that there were a few more things in this room that had originally been concealed from her view because they were against the back of the wall she had just been trying to break through. There was a half-open suitcase on the floor, and the part of the zip that wasn't sealed up allowed Nicola to see a pair of men's trousers poking out from the inside. That was further proof that this room was in use, and Nicola shook her head as she stood there in this murky basement bedroom and thought about how awful it was of Barbara to make her son live in these conditions whenever he was home. But then again, she knew Barbara had never been the best mother to her son and had often used his learning difficulties as a way of treating him terribly and getting away with it. The awful thing was that wasn't even the worst thing the old woman was guilty of.

But right now, Nicola knew she couldn't afford to spend any time feeling sorry for Tony or the living conditions he was put in when he was home. She had to try and get out of here, and the best way of doing that would be if she could get these damn restraints off her wrists and ankles.

Looking at the dresser table, Nicola wondered if there was anything in there that could help her, so she carefully hopped her way over to it, and with her back to it, she used her hands behind her to open the top drawer. Turning back around, she looked into the drawer to see if there was anything there that she could use. But all she saw were a load of black socks, which was more evidence that this room was being used but still no help to her escape attempt.

Bending her knees so that she could open the second drawer, Nicola was once again disappointed when she turned to see what was in that one. Male underwear.

'Come on,' Nicola said under her breath as she refused to believe that there wasn't something in here that she could use to free herself. She had come so far and discovered so much already, having got off the chair, made it to the locked door before discovering this hidden room full of furniture and clothes. The harder she worked, the more she seemed to discover, so that told her that she just had to keep working until she got the lucky break that all her endeavours deserved.

Nicola was just about to give up on the dresser table when she had an idea. What if she was to use the sharp edges of the table to try and cut through the tape on her wrists? If she could get enough momentum, then she could wear through the tape and release her hands, giving her the chance to free her ankles too.

Getting into position with her back to the dresser table, Nicola began rubbing her restraints against the edge of it, dragging the material up and down and hoping that it would slowly but surely start to make inroads in it and cause it to weaken.

Working faster as she became more determined to make this work, Nicola started to feel the pressure lessening around her wrists, and that told her that this was working. The edge of the table was cutting through her restraints. She just had to keep going.

Doing just that, Nicola ignored the loud banging of the table as it rattled against the wall behind it as she kept working, and when the critical moment came for her restraints to snap and her hands to become free, she almost fell to the floor in shock.

She had done it. Now all she had to do was free her ankles, and she would stand a very good chance of being able to overpower Barbara the next time she came through that door.

Sitting on the edge of the bed and untying the restraints from her ankles, Nicola felt the hard, lumpy mattress beneath her and wondered how anybody could sleep on this thing. But she knew that she could expose Barbara once she was out of here and stop her from forcing her son to sleep in this room whenever he was home, not to mention pay for the crimes she had committed against her family today.

Nicola felt a lump in her throat as she thought of her family members and how they had succumbed to whatever Barbara had put in that lemon cake. All she could hope was that whatever sedative they had been given had not killed them and that they were perhaps hurt but okay, and wondering where she was.

Now it was time to get back to them.

With all of her restraints removed, Nicola walked out of the hidden bedroom and over towards the broken chair, where she picked up one of the legs and hit it against her other hand, testing it out to make sure that it was sturdy enough to use as a weapon. This would be the thing that she would hit Barbara over the head with the next time the old woman unlocked that door, so she needed to ensure that it would do the job of knocking her unconscious.

Confident that the chair leg was up to the task she needed it for, Nicola knew now that all she had to do was get Barbara to unlock this door and come and visit her.

Walking over to the door with the chair leg in one hand, Nicola used her free hand to bang on the door and call out Barbara's name.

'Barbara! I can't breathe! You need to open this door!'

It was a lie, but that was hardly going to concern Nicola, who was willing to do and say whatever it took to get out of this basement and back to her family next door.

After that cry of help had gone unanswered, Nicola continued to hammer on the door and make as much noise as she could, shouting out at the top of her lungs and just praying that she was making enough noise for Barbara to have to come down here and shut her up. The prisoner had no idea if the sounds were audible above ground because she didn't know how far down she was, but she hoped that the noise was filtering up because if it was, Barbara would be concerned about any of the other neighbours hearing.

Sure enough, Nicola's prayers were answered when she heard movement on the other side of the door, and as she stepped back away from it and gripped the broken chair leg tightly, she prepared for what she was about to do.

She was only looking to injure and disable Barbara.

But she was prepared to kill if she had to.

The sound of the key turning in the lock told Nicola that her moment to strike was almost here, and as she raised the chair leg above her head, she saw the door opening, and more light flooded into the room.

The brightness caused Nicola to squint as her eyes had to adjust, but as a figure filled the doorway, the prisoner almost dropped the chair leg in shock.

That was because it wasn't Barbara who was entering the room now.

It wasn't even Tony, her son.

It was Bill, the man who was supposed to be dead.

14

1990

Nicola had not complained as much about having to go next door the second time her mum had dropped her off to be babysat. The young girl would still have preferred to not have to go, but she had actually quite enjoyed herself the first time she had been left with the neighbours, so she didn't kick up anywhere near as much of a fuss when Ruth told her it would be happening again. The busy mother was grateful for that as she knocked on Bill and Barbara's front door before she would rush off with her husband to take their son to yet another one of his swimming races, the last of which he had won, so things were looking promising on that front.

Nicola stood beside her mother with her bag full of dolls just like the first time she had come here, only this time she hadn't just brought them because she wanted to. She had also brought them because Barbara had told her to, and Nicola was happy that the woman had shown such an interest in the things that gave the young girl so much joy.

It was Barbara who answered the door this time, and she smiled widely when she saw Nicola waiting to enter her home before welcoming the child in and wishing Ruth a good day. Then she closed the door, and once again, Nicola was back in the quiet and still fairly unfamiliar house. And once again, Barbara had baked a cake.

The first hour had flown by as Nicola had tucked into some ginger cake while Barbara had not only asked her more questions about her dolls, but also shown her some of the dolls she used to play with as a child. While Nicola did not think that Barbara's dolls were anywhere near as nice as the ones she owned, she had been very polite and kept that opinion to herself, instead complimenting the woman on her possessions and spending a little time playing with them as much as the ones she owned. But as the babysitting duties moved into the second hour and the leftover cake was put away, Nicola learnt that this visit was actually going to differ from her first one, after all. That was because Barbara asked her if she would like to go upstairs and see the playroom.

'Yes, please,' Nicola replied, curious and excited in equal measure to see what toys might be in that particular room.

'Follow me then,' Barbara said with a warm smile, and Nicola went to leave the table before looking back at her dolls, almost as if she was hesitant to leave them alone while she was gone.

'Don't worry about them. They'll be fine,' Barbara assured the young girl, and Nicola was trusting enough to separate herself from her precious dolls and leave the kitchen with the homeowner.

Walking back through the hallway, Nicola could hear the sounds from the television in the living room. That was where Bill was, and she knew that because

Barbara had told Nicola that her husband was watching his favourite daytime shows, and he didn't like to be interrupted when that was the case. Nicola didn't think that it was rude of Bill not to have come and said hello to her because she liked television too and knew that it was sometimes better than having to talk to other people, so she passed the living room and followed Barbara up the stairs. But the older woman had only got halfway up when she paused and looked back at Nicola below her before putting her finger to her lips and telling her to be quiet.

Nicola wasn't sure why they had to be quiet, nor did she think that she was being particularly noisy before that warning came, but she followed the orders because she still really wanted to see the playroom.

When they arrived on the upstairs landing, Nicola saw that there were four doors up here, two open, two closed. She didn't know which one would lead into the playroom, but she didn't want to ask either because she knew that she was supposed to be being as quiet as possible.

Barbara walked slowly down the hallway and Nicola followed, and as they passed the first open door, Nicola saw that it looked like a bedroom inside. The second open door showed her a bathroom, but as they reached the first closed door, Barbara again turned around to tell the young girl something.

'This is Tony's room,' Barbara said as she nodded her head towards the closed door they were standing beside. 'But he is not to be disturbed because he is not feeling well today. Okay?'

Nicola nodded her head and hoped that Tony would be feeling better soon because she knew how rubbish it was to be unwell. Being ill meant not getting to play with toys, and while it did mean getting to miss school if that illness fell on a weekday, that wasn't much good if you were ill on a weekend like poor Tony was.

Nicola followed closely behind Barbara as she moved onto the fourth and final door, and the child was excited to see what might be waiting on the other side of it for her. She was hoping that there would be shelves and shelves full of all sorts of toys, but she also hoped that there would be something of interest to her and that Tony didn't just have a load of boring action figurines like her brother had. Nicola and Colin didn't have a playroom in their own house and tended to have to keep their own toys in their own room. But as Barbara opened the door, Nicola felt very excited about being about to enter a room that was specifically designated as a room to play in.

And then she saw it, and to say she was underwhelmed was an understatement.

There were not the rows of shelves full of toys that she had imagined, nor were there any real toys that she could see. All there appeared to be was a small table and chair set in the middle of the room and a large wooden chest in the corner. Maybe that had all the toys in it, Nicola thought as she stared at the chest. That was what she hoped anyway, otherwise it was going to be extremely boring to play in this room, particularly when she had left all her dolls downstairs.

'What do you think?' Barbara asked the young girl as they stood in the doorway and looked around.

Nicola really didn't know what to say, so she just smiled and looked towards the chest again, hoping that Barbara would go over to open it and reveal lots of cool things inside. But Barbara didn't budge. She just stood there as if she was waiting for Nicola to start playing.

But what was she supposed to start playing with?

Nicola looked around the room again as if she must have missed something the first time, but it was still as bland as she had first seen it. There weren't even any pictures or posters on the wall.

If this was a playroom, then it was the worst one she had ever seen.

'Have a seat,' Barbara said as she gestured towards the table and chairs, but Nicola lingered in the doorway because she would much rather just go back downstairs and play with her dolls at the kitchen table again. But Barbara clearly had no plans to return to the kitchen because she walked into the room and stood by the table before beckoning for Nicola to come closer.

Nicola didn't feel like she had much choice, so she stepped into the playroom, and when she reached the table, Barbara pulled out one of the chairs for her.

'Good girl,' she said as the youngster finally sat down, and once she was seated, the older woman walked over to the chest in the corner.

Nicola watched her with interest because she was hoping all of this was going to start making sense and that there would be lots of toys coming out any moment, once that chest was open. Maybe this was just a very tidy playroom, and Tony had to put all his toys away whenever he was finished playing with them, unlike Nicola and Colin, who often left all their things out all over their parents' house during and after their games. But as Barbara crouched down in front of the chest, Nicola was hoping that she might get the chance to make a little bit of a mess now with all the things that were going to come out of it.

Reaching into her pocket, Barbara took out what looked like a small key and then she put it into the lock on the chest as Nicola watched on. The young girl didn't know why the chest was kept locked, but she thought it might mean there was something very special inside and that kept her interested enough to keep watching. But it was at that moment that Barbara turned her back and shielded most of the chest from the girl at the table, and even when she opened the lid, Nicola couldn't see what was inside it. She leaned forward and strained to try and get a glimpse, but she couldn't manage it, and it felt very frustrating for her to be kept in suspense like this.

Finally, Barbara turned around and showed Nicola what she had found in the chest and when she did, the girl felt almost as underwhelmed as when she had first been shown this room.

Barbara had two puppets in her hand, and while they were cute and Nicola was still young, she still felt like she was too old to really be interested in playing with these kinds of things.

‘Say hello to Beatrice and Gordon,’ Barbara said as she proudly held out the puppets so Nicola could get a better look before joining the girl at the table and taking a seat opposite her.

‘Which one would you like to play with first?’ Barbara asked as she placed the puppets on the table in between them.

Nicola looked down at the two options, and while neither of them seemed appealing, she was at least drawn more to one than the other. The one she was looking at with a tiny bit more interest was the red bear with the black button eyes and the smile. The other one was a yellow giraffe, but that just looked very childish, whereas at least the bear looked somewhat more grown-up for a six-year-old like Nicola.

Barbara must have noticed that Nicola was leaning towards picking the red bear because she herself picked it up and held it out towards her.

‘This is Beatrice,’ the woman said. ‘She’s pleased to meet you.’

Nicola accepted the puppet and stared down at its little face.

‘Put her on your hand,’ Barbara instructed her. ‘She’s a puppet, so that’s the best place for her.’

Nicola did just that, putting her hand inside the puppet until her fingers had slotted into each of the holes cut inside Beatrice’s head and arms. Then she wriggled her fingers, and sure enough, the puppet came alive.

‘Wonderful,’ Barbara said as she watched Nicola playing with Beatrice before she picked up the giraffe and put that on her own hand. 'We can play together now.'

With that, Barbara began moving her hand around and wriggling her fingers so that it looked like the giraffe, or Gordon as he was known, was alive and being playful.

Making the giraffe's long neck go up and down, Barbara pretended to make the puppet nibble on Beatrice, which caused Nicola to smile and move her own puppet out of the way. She still wasn't thrilled to be playing with puppets because they definitely weren't as much fun as her dolls downstairs, but she was at least enjoying having somebody to play a game with. Her brother never played with her at home, and her parents were often too busy to give her as much time as she wanted, but Barbara seemed fully engaged in being with Nicola and trying to make her enjoy herself.

But as Barbara continued to control Gordon enthusiastically, Nicola glanced over towards the chest, wondering if there was anything else in there that might be more interesting to her than these puppets.

'What are you doing?' Barbara suddenly asked her, stopping her own puppet and looking very serious.

'Nothing,' Nicola said quickly, looking away from the chest and back to the puppet on her hand, but it was too late. Barbara had already sensed that the girl was bored.

'Are you having fun?' she asked Nicola.

'Yes, I am,' Nicola lied, not wanting to hurt Barbara's feelings because she was a sweet girl, and she knew even at her tender age that it was not nice to upset somebody.

'You don't look like you are.'

'I am. It's just…'

'What?'

'I'd rather play with my dolls if that's okay.'

Barbara stared at Nicola for a moment before she took her puppet off her hand and placed it down on the table again. Then she shrugged her shoulders and stood up.

'Where are you going?' Nicola asked Barbara as the woman walked towards the door.

'I'm going to get my husband,' Barbara replied.

'Why?'

'Because it's time for him to play with us too.'

With that, Barbara left the room, and Nicola was alone with only Beatrice and Gordon for company. But they weren't much fun, so she took her puppet off her hand and placed it down beside the giraffe before getting up from her seat and going over to the chest to see if there was anything else inside.

But when she got there, she looked down to see that there were no toys inside. There was only a large book, and when Nicola picked it up, she opened it up to see that it was a photo album.

Turning the pages, Nicola saw that the pictures in here were of other children, but she didn't recognise any of them. But she did recognise something. She recognised the puppets that the children had on their hands.

She recognised Beatrice.

Looking at the faces of the children, Nicola noticed that none of the kids were smiling. They were all just either staring glumly at the camera or not even looking at all, some with their heads bowed as if they were shy or just didn't want to have their picture taken. But before Nicola could look at any more photos, the album was snatched from her hand, and when she looked up, she saw that it was Bill who had taken it from her.

'This isn't for you to look at,' the man said firmly before putting the album back in the chest and asking Barbara to lock it up.

She did as she was told as Bill went and took a seat at the table, and he made sure that Nicola knew she was to join him.

Nicola was reluctant to go and sit back down because she didn't really want to play with the puppets again, and she didn't really want to stay here in this boring room. But Bill told her to sit, and his tone of voice made her too afraid to say no.

As she joined the man at the table, Barbara walked over to the door, and it looked like she was going to leave.

'Where are you going?' Nicola asked, hoping that she wasn't going to be left alone with Bill because she didn't know him as well as she knew Barbara and would much rather play with the woman than this rather grumpy man. But Barbara didn't answer her. She didn't say a word at all. She just looked back over her shoulder at the young girl before pulling the door closed and leaving her alone with her husband.

15

PRESENT DAY

The sight of the old man standing in the doorway was shocking to Nicola on many levels. First and foremost, it was shocking because he was supposed to have died earlier this year. That's what Nicola's parents had told her, and it was also what Barbara had confirmed at the dinner table.

He had died of a heart attack. Barbara was a widow now.

Or at least that was how the story went.

But somehow, that was not the truth, and this couple had clearly been able to deceive other people into thinking that was the case. But why? What could they possibly stand to gain from faking his death? But those answers would hopefully come in time. It was the second reason for Nicola's shock that made this even more of a tense situation. That's because this was the first time Nicola had properly come face to face with the man who had sexually abused her in a very, very long time.

Nicola had been six years old when she had found herself in some very traumatic situations, but it had been many years later before she had truly been able to understand the gravity of what she had been through, as well as the depths of evil that the couple next door had plunged to. Bill and Barbara weren't just the friendly neighbours that everybody thought they were. They were vile, despicable people who did not deserve to be breathing. But here they were, both breathing, and after one of them was supposed to have died as well.

That was why Nicola wasn't able to use the chair leg as a weapon in the end. She was too stunned and too caught off guard with seeing the man in front of her that all she could do was stand there helplessly and stare back into the wrinkled face of the man before her.

But as she did, she realised something. She realised that Bill, even though he was alive, was not exactly in the best of health. His face was more drawn and haggard than his wife's, and he was leaning against the side of the doorway almost as if he needed to use it for support. He was skinny but not in a healthy way, and his breathing also sounded a little laboured, like he was still trying to get it under control after coming down here and opening this door. But there was still something about him that Nicola recognised from the past.

The light in his eyes when he looked at her was still there, and that meant that despite everything, this was still very much the same person who had taken pleasure in hurting her.

'What's the matter, dear?' Barbara said as she stepped out from behind her husband and into the basement in front of him. 'You look as if you've seen a ghost.'

'You're supposed to be dead,' Nicola muttered as she kept staring at the old man in the doorway. 'How?'

Bill didn't answer that question, and it was Barbara who spoke again.

'Don't worry. You're not the only one to have been fooled by our little trick. Everyone else believes that my husband is dead too. You're now one of the very select few people who know the truth.'

'Why?' Nicola asked, her voice barely audible as she found it difficult to muster any kind of inner strength to project her voice properly.

'It's a long story, but I'd be more than happy to tell you it, seeing as we're going to be spending rather a lot of time together down here. But first of all, how about you put down that chair leg?'

Barbara eyed the potential weapon in Nicola's hand, and that was the thing that reminded the younger woman that she was still holding it. But now she had been snapped back into reality, there was no way she was going to give it up that easily. Despite the shock of everything that had just happened, Nicola could still see that these two people were frail and most likely much weaker than she was. Yes, they had hurt her, but that had been back when she had been the vulnerable one. But now she had grown up, and these two had aged a lot. That was why she didn't let go of the chair leg and instead chose to raise it above her head again in preparation to strike.

She was still determined to fight her way out of here.

Barbara realised that too, which was perhaps why she quickly stepped back towards where she had just come from and intimated that her husband should do the same. But Nicola didn't care if they were trying to retreat. If anything, that was a good sign. At least it was until she saw the real reason why Barbara and her husband had taken a backwards step.

It was so they could allow somebody else into the room.

It was Tony, their son.

Nicola hesitated when she saw the stocky man fill the frame of the door, and that urgent desire of hers to push forward and attack was thwarted somewhat by her realisation that there was no way she would be able to overpower him. Tony wasn't elderly and frail, or susceptible to speed and a vicious need for vengeance. He was the same age as Nicola, but he was bigger and more powerful, so it made her chances of success in attacking him smaller.

Yet despite his connection to the two monsters who had brought him into this world, he was not someone Nicola wished to hurt. That was because Tony had never done anything wrong to her during those ill-fated babysitting visits in her youth. In fact, she had barely seen him during those times because he was usually locked away in his bedroom. If anything, Nicola suspected he had also been a victim of his parents' disgusting desires, and she had often wondered how much his limited mental capabilities had given his mum and dad the opportunity to abuse him and get away with it more easily than they had done with her. That was why Nicola paused and kept her weapon a safe distance away from him.

She wanted to see if he was here to help her.

She wanted to know if he had suffered just as much as she had.

But then Tony made it clear that while he might have suffered the same, if not more than Nicola, he was still very much on the side of his parents because he told Nicola to put the chair leg down too.

'Help me get out of here,' Nicola pleaded with him desperately before she followed any orders. 'You can help me. You know this is wrong.'

But Tony just stared at Nicola and waited for her to do what he had asked.

'Please, Tony! Help me!' she begged again. 'Your parents are cruel, but you're not like them. You're like me. And we're friends, remember?'

Nicola was hoping that by referencing their one and only very brief interaction as children that she might somehow be able to make this man pick her over the couple standing behind him. But calling themselves friends was a bit of a reach, and the conversation that Nicola was hinting at had occurred over thirty years ago, so she didn't even know if Tony remembered them being friendly towards each other. And then she got her confirmation, not just of the fact he didn't remember it, but also that this was a man who had health issues of his own, just like his frail father behind him. It was just that those issues were mainly consigned to his mind rather than his body.

'I want to play with Nicola,' Tony said, turning to look at his mother behind him as if he was a child asking for her permission.

'Not now, Tony,' Barbara said before ordering him to take the chair leg off the young woman but to be careful in doing so.

Tony looked back at Nicola before shrugging his shoulders and stepping towards her, clearly following instructions and demonstrating just how strong the parent-child bond still was here. He might have been a grown man, but he was still very much under the control of those who had raised him.

As he got closer to her, Nicola spotted the top of a pair of scissors sticking out from the front pocket of his jeans. That was precisely the kind of weapon she could make good use of in here, either to attack or if she was to find herself with her hands tied again, but she had no idea how she would ever be able to get the scissors from the man.

'Tony, please,' Nicola tried as he got closer to her, and she feared she was going to have to try and hurt him if he kept coming nearer. To show that, she gripped the chair leg even tighter and pulled back her arm to make it look like she was prepared to strike. But still Tony kept coming. Still, he was supporting his parents over her.

That was why Nicola had no choice in the end.

She had to do what she did.

She had to hit him.

Bringing the chair leg down as hard as she could, she struck Tony on his left shoulder, and when she did, the leg snapped clean in half, and she lost her grip on the end she had been holding. But that wasn't all that happened. Tony howled out in pain and appeared genuinely hurt, and while she had hit him hard, his reaction was not that of a man his age. Instead, it was that of a child, and he turned to look back at his parents with tears in his eyes.

'Mummy, it hurts,' Tony told Barbara, and the old woman glared at Nicola, not believing that she had dared to strike her son. But she had done it, and there was no taking it back now. Nor was there much she could do about trying to strike again because the chair leg was in pieces on the floor, and she had nothing else to hit him with other than her fists, which were hardly likely to do much damage.

'What do we do to bullies?' Barbara asked her son, and Tony nodded his head before turning back to Nicola, and through his tear-stained eyes, the woman saw a rage beginning to build. And that did not bode well for her.

'I'm sorry!' Nicola cried, putting her hands out in front of herself before Tony could do anything that might hurt her. 'I just want to go home. I just want to see my family. You understand that, don't you?'

She maintained her defensive demeanour as she waited to see what Tony would say to that. But he said nothing, instead just rubbing his sore shoulder and still appearing in pain.

'I just want to see my mummy and daddy,' Nicola said, using language she felt he might be more susceptible to. 'Please, just let me go and see them. I'm sorry I hurt you, but I'm just scared.'

Tony suddenly seemed unsure again, so he did what he always seemed to do in these situations and looked to his mother for guidance. But she was not as undecided as him, and she made that clear by telling him to shut Nicola up because all this arguing was upsetting Bill.

The emotion of his father seemed to be the factor in getting Tony to finally act because he rushed over to Nicola and grabbed her, putting one hand over her mouth as his other hand pushed her towards the wall. As she bumped into the brickwork, Nicola moaned in pain before Tony let go, and she lowered herself to the floor in an effort to make herself a smaller target and less easy to hold on to. But that seemed to suit Barbara just fine.

'Now you sit here, and you stay quiet,' the old woman said. 'Or Tony will hurt you, and he'll hurt you a lot more than you hurt him.'

Nicola wanted to speak and get some answers, even if she was realising that she was not going to get out of this room, but Tony was still standing over her, and his fists were clenched, meaning she didn't want to risk doing anything that might draw his ire, or his mother's.

'Come and help your father into bed,' Barbara told her son, and he sprang into action, rushing over to Bill and putting his arm around his weary father, who was still yet to speak a single word before helping him move forward in the direction of the secret bedroom down here.

Nicola watched as the two men passed by in front of her, shuffling slowly forward and proving just how much weaker Bill was now than the last time she had seen him. It wasn't clear what his health issue was, but he was certainly dependent on the assistance of his other family members, and by the time Tony had got him into the secret room and put him into bed, the old man looked absolutely exhausted.

'What's wrong with him?' Nicola asked Barbara, who had remained standing by the doorway.

'None of your business,' she snapped back before pointing towards the wall and the hole that Nicola had created. 'I see you managed to find his bedroom before I showed it to you. That's disappointing.'

'Why is he living down here?' Nicola asked.

'Why do you think? The whole world thinks he's dead, so he can hardly be walking around on the streets and going into the pub for a pint, can he?'

Nicola still couldn't fathom why this man would need to fake his own death and stay hidden away down here, but even something as bizarre as that was the least of her concerns right now.

'Please just tell me if my family are okay?' Nicola asked. 'I just want to know they are okay.'

'I bet you do. But I'm afraid you won't be seeing your family again. Well, most of them anyway.'

Nicola's chest tightened, and her breath caught in her throat as she processed what Barbara had just said to her.

'What do you mean? What have you done to them?'

Scrambling to her feet, Nicola was just about to rush at the old woman and try to get some answers, but Tony was on hand to catch up and hold her back before she could get to her.

‘Tell me!’ Nicola cried as Tony pulled her back away from the door. ‘What have you done?’

But Barbara did not speak to Nicola again. All she did was leave the room for a moment before returning with the roll of duct tape. But this time she wasn’t put on a chair. She was taken into the corner and pushed to the floor before her hands and legs were tied so tightly that she could barely move a muscle. Then Barbara told Tony that the wall would need to be repaired but that they had other work to do first before the pair left the room and locked the door, leaving Nicola tied up in this basement again.

Only this time, she wasn’t completely alone.

Bill was with her now, and as she looked over at him in his bed, she saw something that made her feel physically sick.

The old man was smiling at her.

16

1990

'Are you okay?' Ruth asked her daughter as she observed her chewing her food in a very quiet fashion.

Nicola nodded her head and just kept eating, having not said anything at all since this meal began, which was the main reason why Ruth had asked her daughter the question in the first place. This little girl was many things, but one thing she never seemed to be was quiet. Yet she was practically mute now and had been at several of the other family meals this week. Not only that, but Nicola had not been acting in her usual manner, which tended to involve her stomping around the house making as much mess and noise as possible. But Nicola had spent most of her free time over these last few days in her bedroom, and whenever her parents had gone to check on her, they had found her either lying on her bed pretending to be asleep or just sitting and staring at some of her dolls without actually picking them up and playing with them.

'Has something happened at school?' John asked his daughter, sharing the concern his wife felt for their child's recent change in behaviour.

But Nicola again just shook her head and stared at her plate, and while the food on it did not seem to be going down very fast, Nicola herself felt keen to be able to get down from this table and go back to her bedroom, and she told her parents as much. But they were not having it.

'Finish your food first,' Ruth told her, and Nicola sighed before picking up her fork and scooping up some more of the peas that she usually chomped down eagerly.

Nicola took a while to eat what was on her plate, but she managed it, all without saying a word as her parents sat beside her and shared a few more troubled looks. Her brother, Colin, had already left the table after finishing his meal ten minutes ago, being allowed to leave so that he could go and play on his games console again. But even clearing her plate was not enough for Nicola to be allowed to go, despite what her parents had just told her, and as she put down her knife and fork, Ruth spoke again.

'Darling, we're very worried about you,' she said. 'Are you sure there isn't something that's bothering you?'

Nicola didn't know what to do because while there was something troubling her, she was scared to talk about it. That was why she just shook her head again and said that everything was fine.

In the end, John and Ruth didn't see what else they could do other than to allow their daughter to leave the dining table, and the young girl made her way back to her bedroom feeling sad because she could see that her parents were worried about her. But she had been able to keep the secret that Bill and Barbara had told her she had to keep, and because of that, she was confident that she wasn't going to get in any trouble.

Nicola felt slightly better once she had closed her bedroom door and crawled onto her bed because she felt safe in here where she was alone and where no adult could tell her what to do. If it was up to her, she would stay in here a lot more, but she still had to go to school. She also still had to keep going next door whenever her parents took her brother swimming.

The thought of being back in the playroom with the puppets made Nicola feel uncomfortable, but she felt even worse when she thought about what would happen if she tried to tell her mum and dad that she no longer wished to go there. They would want to know why, and what could she say to that? She would either have to lie, which would get her in trouble, or she would have to tell the truth, which would also get her in trouble. That meant it was easier to just keep going and not cause anybody any problems. She just wished that she could be left alone at Bill and Barbara's, or at least just be allowed to sit in the kitchen and eat cake with her dolls like she had done the first couple of times she had been left there. What she didn't like was having to play with Bill in that playroom because he was not quite as nice as his wife, and he was always telling Nicola what to do, rather than asking her if she wanted to do it. He was weird, and it had been a lot better when he had just stayed in the living room, watching TV by himself.

Things had definitely got worse ever since he had started getting involved in playtime.

But she knew she wasn't the only one who had to play those games with Bill. Barbara had told her that Eric, the young boy who also lived on this street, had partaken in the puppet games, and he had not complained or told anybody the secret, so the implication was that Nicola should do the same. Therefore, she had, but that didn't mean she felt much better about it all.

Nicola didn't understand why she was feeling so upset all the time, she just knew that she was scared. She was scared of Bill and Barbara and the secret they were making her keep, and she was also scared of being a naughty girl for her mum and dad. She had never used to worry about that second thing and had instead always just let her personality come out in a carefree fashion. But after her neighbours had told her how important it was for her to be good, she had changed her behaviour. She had done that because Bill and Barbara had told her that not being good would mean that she would never be allowed out to see her friends, just like their son, Tony, was now.

The young boy that lived next door was still a mystery to Nicola because she had been kept away from him whenever she had been there, or rather, he had been kept away from her. Despite always asking if she could play with somebody her own age, Bill and Barbara had continued to deny her the chance to go into Tony's bedroom and see the boy. Whenever she asked them why that was, they had just told her that their son had been naughty and that he wasn't to play with other children until he was being better behaved again. Nicola figured that whatever he had done must have been really bad for him to be in trouble for so long, but she still had no idea what it was. She really wanted to know, if only so she could make sure that she never did that same thing and got locked away herself for that much time.

It wasn't even as if Nicola could see Tony at school and talk to him there because he went to a different school than she did. Her parents said it was a special school for children who need a little extra help with their work, and while Nicola didn't know if that meant Tony was smarter than her or not as much, she was curious about where he got to spend his time. But it was just one more thing she couldn't talk to him about because she never got to see him.

Lying on her bed and thinking about what her next visit to Bill and Barbara's house might be like, she wondered if it would go the same way as her last visit. That had been where she had played another game of hand puppets with Bill, and he had made her feel weird, not at all like how any other adult usually made her feel when she played with them. She was always having to beg her parents to play with her, and even when they did, it was obvious they weren't as interested in the games as she was. But the couple next door seemed to love playing games, or rather, they loved playing one specific game, and Nicola wondered why they were so hard on their son if that was the case.

Were they choosing to play with her so much because they couldn't play with Tony? Were they using her to make him feel bad about not getting to come out and play himself? Or did Bill and Barbara just really like playing games? If so, why didn't they have more toys in that chest in the playroom?

Why was it always the hand puppets, and why was Bill always telling Nicola what the rules of the game were instead of letting her just play her own way?

Nicola often argued with her parents, but she felt like her daddy was much nicer than Tony's was. John was nice, but Bill could be mean, especially if she said she didn't want to do something. She also felt like Ruth was better than Barbara, even if Barbara did bake really nice cakes. She felt that way because her mum always made her feel good, whereas sometimes, Barbara only made her feel good if it was to get her to do something she had originally not wanted to do.

Hearing her brother's shout from the next bedroom, Nicola recognised it as the thing her sibling often did whenever he was celebrating doing something that had happened on his video game. He was always playing that game, just like he was always going swimming. And most of all, he was always happy.

Nicola used to be that way too. She used to love playing with her dolls and making lots of noises. But now she was different, and she knew why that was. It was because her brother didn't have to go next door.

Only she did.

Only she was the one who had been told to keep a secret.

And she was going to keep it.

She was going to keep it for a very long time.

17

PRESENT DAY

In all the time she had been sitting in this basement looking across at the old man in the bed, Nicola hadn't been able to bring herself to say anything. That very much reminded her of how she used to behave around this man when she was six years old and alone with him in that playroom. She had stopped speaking to him after he had done things to her, and she had not spoken to him since as she had grown up in the house next door and avoided having to be babysat as Colin's Saturday swimming races petered out, and there was no need for her to be left with the neighbours.

But not only had Nicola not spoken to Bill in all this time about what had happened, she hadn't spoken to anybody. Not a single soul, other than Bill and Barbara, knew exactly what had occurred when she had been left here as a child. It was possible that Tony knew, although Nicola didn't know that for sure, and as far as she could guess, he could have been as much of a victim as she was. Therefore, there were only three people in this world who truly knew what had gone on, and up to a couple of hours ago, Nicola thought that number had reduced to two. But Bill was still very much alive, and although he was hardly in the greatest of health, the fact he was still able to stare and smile at Nicola from his secretive hidey-hole in the basement of this house was extremely difficult for her. But as bad as that was, it wasn't as bad as the thought that she might never be able to see her family again.

From what Barbara had intimated, that would be the case. Nicola wouldn't see any of them again, although she still didn't know why. Was that because they were all dead? Or was it because she was going to be dead herself very soon? Neither of those possibilities were bearable, but what could she do other than sit down here and wait to find out? She was tied up better this time, so another attempt at an escape was off the cards. That, coupled with the fact that she was now in the presence of a man who could make her feel weaker than any other person she had ever been around before, meant that she was hardly feeling in the right frame of mind to be aggressive and decisive.

Despite being a lot older than she had been when she had been alone with Bill as a child, she still felt the power he had over her.

She still felt just as helpless as before.

Perhaps it had been a good thing that Bill had seemingly lost the use of his voice because it meant that he wasn't able to talk to her either. That meant there was no taunting or terrorising, although he was still doing a fairly good job of that with the strength of the smile on his face. It might have seemed strange for a man as fragile as him, who was living in a basement, to seem happy about things, but Bill was certainly managing it. But what was he happy about? The fact that Nicola was back in his life? Or the fact that whatever crazy plan he and his wife had conjured up was actually working?

The sound of the key in the lock came sometime later, long after Nicola had lost even more sense of time and well before she could have hoped to have felt tired enough to enjoy a couple of minutes of peaceful sleep. But when it did, it was soon to be followed by something Nicola had been desperately seeking ever since this ordeal had begun.

The truth.

Barbara entered the room alone this time with her son nowhere to be seen, which told the prisoner two things. One, she was obviously feeling confident enough now that Nicola had no way of trying to escape so as not to need the extra protection. And two, that her one and only potential ally in this house was no longer present, leaving Nicola with her two enemies and people whom she knew had never had her best interests at heart from the first moment they had met her.

Barbara went and took a seat in the chair beside her husband's bed but made sure that she was still visible through the doorway of the artificial bedroom so that Nicola could see her from where she was sitting in the corner of the basement.

'Please tell me what you have done to my family,' Nicola asked in a low voice, and to her surprise, she got an answer.

'Your family are alive,' Barbara replied, and Nicola felt relief flooding through her entire body. But that moment of optimism was quickly washed out by what came next.

'But very soon, they will be gone, perishing in a terrible house fire, a fire in which there will be no survivors, or at least that's what the police will believe anyway.'

Nicola stared in horror at the old woman by the bed, disbelieving of the craziness of what she had just heard.

'What the hell are you talking about?'

'My little trick with the lemon cake just sedated them, and they are still sleeping now. That has allowed Tony enough time to position their bodies upstairs in the bedrooms, where it will look like they were sleeping peacefully until a fire ripped through the home, and they succumbed to the smoke before they had a chance to even think about escaping.'

The calm manner in which Barbara laid out her plan was almost as chilling as the plan itself, and Nicola felt as scared of the woman in the basement as she did at the thought of what was about to happen to her family.

'Don't worry, you will be joining your relatives shortly, enjoying your own peaceful slumber before your life leaves this Earth.'

'Why?' Nicola had to know. 'Why do you want to kill us all?'

'I didn't say I wanted to kill you all,' Barbara said with a knowing smile, and she looked at her husband before chuckling. 'The fire will be so severe, and the bodies so badly burned, that it will be difficult to really know exactly who was in the house at the time. That means nobody will know that somebody actually survived the fire. Little Ben, your gorgeous nephew, will be spared death, and while the outside world will mourn him, he will actually live on, here, in this house, with me and my husband.'

It was at that moment that Nicola realised the true terrifying scale of this couple's plan. They weren't just two people who had abused a child in their past. They were two people who were desperately seeking another opportunity to do so, only this time, they would not be limited by how often they could do such a thing. They wouldn't need a local neighbourhood kid to be left in their care for a couple of hours while the parents were busy elsewhere. If this worked, they would have a little boy all to themselves for as long as they wanted it.

'No!' Nicola cried, trying to get up but finding it impossible with her legs bound together as they were. 'You can't do this! You can't hurt him!'

'We're not going to hurt him,' Barbara said before looking to her husband. 'Are we, Bill?'

Bill shook his head and displayed that galling grin of his, the one Nicola had already been subjected to far too many times in her life.

'Please don't do this,' Nicola pleaded. 'You know it's wrong. You know it will hurt him, and he's not as strong as I am.'

'Well, he doesn't have to be,' Barbara snapped back. 'He doesn't have to keep a secret like you did. After all, no one will know he is here. Therefore, there is no one he can tell.'

'You're crazy! What makes you think you can get away with this?'

'Because we've already got away with so much,' Barbara replied, and that quick answer was a testament to the confidence that the old woman had, a confidence that Nicola picked up on and found even more disturbing. 'We got away with what we did to you, and we've got away with faking Bill's death, so why can't we do this? Tell me, dear, what is stopping us?'

Nicola really wished that she had a good answer for that question, but she didn't. Despite how bad what these people wanted to do was, she didn't know how she could stop it or how they could get caught by anybody else. But then Nicola thought about what Barbara had just said about her faking her husband's death, and she still had no idea why the couple had needed to do that.

'What did you do?' Nicola wanted to know as she looked at Bill. 'What did you do that was so bad that you had to fake your own death?'

Nicola was terrified of what the answer to that question might be, but she had to know, however bad it may be. That's because she figured there was only one thing she could do at this moment in time and that was keep Barbara down here talking to her for as long as possible. Maybe that way, she was buying the time she needed for somebody to call at her family's house and discover that something was terribly wrong before it was too late.

'Not everybody was like you,' Barbara told Nicola after taking a moment to decide how best to answer that. 'Not everybody could keep a secret like you could.'

Nicola realised what the old woman was getting at, and that meant she figured another poor child had been subjected to the abuse that she herself had suffered in the past, although she had already figured that out in later life after recalling the time she had found the photo album in the playroom.

But had this particular victim been different? Had they told somebody what happened to them instead of carrying the secret shame with them forever?

'His name is Ryan, and he is five years old, or at least he was when we first met him. I first met his mother at church. It was a couple of years ago now. We got talking, as one does, and she told me about how she was praying for her son to be better behaved because it seemed like he was being quite the nuisance for his mum and dad. I told her that she needed a lot more than just prayer to get a child to behave, and when she asked me what I meant, I told her about my own experience, both with my own son and other people's children whom I had looked after.'

Nicola listened on as Barbara told the sorry story, unsure how it was going to end but knowing that it couldn't possibly be good.

'Anyway, we became friendly and would speak with each other every week as we attended the services, and I would always ask her how little Ryan was getting along. Well, one day, she told me that she was reaching the end of her tether with him and felt like she was struggling to cope. That's when I offered my services to her. I told her that I would be happy to watch Ryan for a couple of hours if she ever felt like she needed a break, and eventually, she accepted my invitation.'

Nicola shook her head as she thought about that poor boy being left in this house, as well as the poor mother who had no idea of the mistake she was making in allowing it to happen.

'Ryan was a nice young boy, but like his mother had warned me, he was a little bit of a nuisance,' Barbara went on. 'But regardless of that, I made sure to show him the playroom and the hand puppets that you used to play with all those years ago. And it kept him entertained, for a little while at least. It kept him entertained until Bill was ready to play with him.'

Nicola knew exactly what that meant, and she felt nauseous as she imagined another innocent child going through what she had been through. But based on how the story had started, it had sounded like this had been one child that had broken the rules of the game.

'What happened?' Nicola wanted to know. 'Did he tell somebody what you did to him?'

'Unfortunately so,' Barbara replied with a shake of her head. 'Despite the warnings we gave him, the stupid little boy went and told his parents what had happened. That meant the police came calling, and when they did, they had a lot of questions to ask Bill.'

'How did you get away with it?' Nicola asked, hoping that the police didn't take just take the perpetrator's word over the victim's.

'We didn't,' Barbara replied rather honestly. 'The police didn't believe Bill, and it became clear that charges were going to be pressed against him. Ryan's family wanted to drag my husband through the courts. They were making out like he was some kind of a monster.'

'Because he is!' Nicola cried. 'You can't do what you did to us and pretend like it's alright. It's illegal, and it's wrong, and you're just as bad as he is, even if you always left the room before the actual abuse started!'

'Calm down, my dear, because I'll tell you right now that if you continue to shout then this conversation will be over, and so will the lives of most of the people you hold dear.'

That ominous warning quickly shut Nicola up, and she kept quiet until Barbara spoke again.

'Bill had suffered a stroke a few months before the police started looking into him, and it had left him very unwell, as you can see now,' Barbara said as she looked sadly at her frail husband beside her. 'I knew that he wasn't healthy enough to go through a trial, never mind whatever sentence he might get at the end of it. That was why I had to do something. I had to fight to save my family just like you're fighting to save yours now.'

Barbara took Bill's hand and gave it a squeeze as Nicola watched on and wondered how she could not only have got away with whatever plan she came up with, but how she could justify it as being the right thing to do.

'I found a man on the internet who offered a rather unusual service,' Barbara confessed. 'He could make it look like somebody had died, and he was very good. Death certificate. Funeral arrangements. Even a headstone in the local cemetery. He could sort it all out for me, for a price, obviously, and if he did that, I knew the investigation into my husband would stop. After all, the police can't prosecute a dead man, can they?'

Nicola could scarcely believe what she was hearing, but it seemed that everything that came out of Barbara's mouth in this basement was unbelievable. She had faked her own husband's death to stop him going to prison for child abuse crimes, meaning the poor victim's family never got the justice they deserved. If only Nicola had her hands free now then she knew exactly what she would do, and it was something she should have done a long time ago.

She would get justice, for herself and for all the other children, however many there had been.

She would get it by killing both of these evil people, and she would do it with her bare hands if she had to.

But she couldn't because her hands were tightly tied together, as were her legs, and that meant all she could do was sit and listen to this awful story and observe how pleased Barbara and Bill seemed to be with themselves for pulling off what they clearly felt like was the con of the century.

'That's why Bill is down here,' Barbara said in conclusion. 'He is hidden away because the world thinks he is dead, and he is hidden away just like Ben will be very shortly. But as you can see, there is still life in the old dog yet, and I will make sure that my husband enjoys however long he actually does have left on this Earth by keeping him in the presence of someone that will fill his last days with joy.'

Now that Nicola had heard everything, she could have been forgiven for giving up all hope and wanting to be put out of her misery, considering all the terrible things she had just learnt had either happened or were about to happen. But deep down, she knew she couldn't do that. She couldn't give up. She had to keep fighting, if not for her and the rest of her family, then for Ben because he was still an innocent child who had been unharmed by these two monsters.

But how could she do it?

How could she get out of this situation?

The way she saw it, she only had one option. She had to see Tony again. She had to appeal to the side of him that wasn't pure evil like his parents were.

That was her only hope now.

But just like it had been when she was a child, it wouldn't be easy to get close to Tony.

18

1990

Nicola didn't say a word as her mother knocked on the door at Bill and Barbara's house for what was supposedly the last time she would be left here to be babysat. Ruth and John were taking Colin for another swimming race, but after the young boy had expressed a desire to no longer give up his Saturdays to spend in the pool, the family had agreed this would be the final trip to the local leisure centre. Colin was going to explore other hobbies after today, or maybe he would just spend his Saturdays playing video games at home, and because of that, Nicola wouldn't have to go next door to be looked after by the neighbours any longer.

That was, of course, a huge relief to the young girl who had very quietly and very defiantly endured what had been a traumatic time for her, and as the door opened and Barbara smiled at her once again, she knew she wouldn't have to keep faking for much longer. Nicola felt that the secret of what she had experienced in this house would be much easier to keep once she was no longer around Bill and Barbara on a weekly basis, and she rather naively believed that her feelings about it all would improve over time.

As she stepped inside the home and waved goodbye to her mother, she had no idea that the pain of what she had been through in this house would last a lifetime and that it was already something that meant her life would never be the same again.

By now, Nicola had been coming here long enough to know that the formalities with the cake in the kitchen were over, and Barbara wasted no time in marching her straight up to the playroom where Bill could play his latest 'game' with her. Just like all the other times, it was deeply troubling for thc young girl, and she couldn't wait for it to be over so that the man would leave her alone, and she could just count down the minutes until her mother came to collect her again. But that time, the ordeal lasted a lot longer than it usually did, perhaps because Bill knew this was the last opportunity he would have to babysit the young girl next door. It lasted so long that Nicola had been unable to stop the tears when they had started flowing, even though she knew that crying was not something that Bill looked fondly on. But she couldn't help it. She just wanted the suffering to stop.

Eventually it did.

But the damage was done long before that.

After Bill had left the playroom, the usual routine was for Barbara to enter and remind the young girl of her obligation to keep the secret before tidying up the puppets and telling Nicola to go to the bathroom to refresh. But as Nicola left the playroom and headed for the bathroom, she decided that today, she was going to do something that went against tradition.

She wasn't just going to go to the bathroom.

She was going to try and see Tony.

Because she knew this might be her last chance to check on the boy and see his room, Nicola felt emboldened enough to take a risk, and she proved it by wrapping her fingers around the door handle to the boy's bedroom and giving it a twist.

Contrary to what Barbara had told her before, the door was not locked, and because of that, Nicola was able to look inside the bedroom and see the occupant sitting on the floor.

Tony looked up at her, surprised and a little scared when he saw Nicola standing in the doorway, and for a second, it looked as though he was going to shout out to alert his parents to the fact that he had an intruder in his room. But Nicola quickly put her finger to her lips, and it told him to stay quiet, a suggestion he followed, which allowed Nicola to close the bedroom door behind her and walk deeper into the room.

Looking around, Nicola saw that this room did seem to have a lot more toys in it than the playroom did, which was promising because she had almost been imagining Tony sitting in a bare bedroom with nothing to do all day. As it was, the bedroom looked fairly normal, which was a relief because as Nicola knew, there wasn't too much about this house that was normal.

'What are you doing?' Tony asked her, taking her attention away from the shelves of figurines and back to him sitting on the floor with a train track circling around him.

'I just want to play,' Nicola replied, and she hoped that would be an answer that Tony would be happy with. But she was wrong.

'You're not allowed in here,' the boy told her. 'You're going to get me in trouble.'

Nicola could tell from his tone of voice that he was genuinely concerned about running afoul of his parents, but was it just himself that he was worried about, or was he worried about her too? How much trouble would she really get in if she was caught in here? Nicola didn't necessarily want to put that to the test, but her curiosity had got the better of her.

'What are you playing?' she asked Tony as she looked down at the train set that surrounded him.

'Trains,' he replied before going back to moving one of the toy trains up and down the wooden track in front of him, seemingly having suddenly forgotten that Nicola's presence here might be a problem.

'Can I play with you?' she asked him, and he nodded his head, so she knelt down beside him and picked up one of the trains.

As she placed it on the track and started following the train that Tony was controlling, it would have been easy for her to feel like this was just a normal playdate with another child her age. But Nicola could still feel that sense of unease that she had felt ever since she had first come here, and despite trying to distract herself with an innocent game, she still felt like something bad was going to happen.

She stopped playing with the train and looked at Tony because she had a question for him.

She wanted to know something.

She wanted to know if Bill and Barbara were making him keep a secret too.

'Do you ever play with the puppets?' she asked him, broaching the subject that way because it was the only way her little mind could think of putting it into a sentence.

Tony stopped moving his train across the track immediately and looked up at Nicola, and even though he didn't speak, it was obvious that he knew what she meant. It was still obvious even when he shook his head a moment later and went back to playing. It had been obvious because he had just gone from looking happy to looking very sad.

'Have you ever told anybody the secret?' Nicola asked him once she felt confident that Tony shared that same secret with her but, again, the young boy just shook his head and went back to playing.

Nicola didn't know what to do, and as she looked at Tony playing in front of her, she could almost feel the sadness seeping out of him. But from this vantage point on the carpet, she could also see under Tony's bed, and when she did, she noticed there were a few more toys under there.

'Do you want to play something else?' she asked him, having spied what looked like a toy shopping basket filled with pretend supermarket items. It looked just like one of the toys Nicola had at home, where she would play in her bedroom and pretend like she was shopping before going to her mother, who would act as the checkout lady, beeping each item before she paid for it with pretend money.

Tony looked under the bed too, and it seemed like he was interested in playing a new game, and he proved it when he pulled out a four-foot long toy that looked a little creepy as it appeared from under the bed.

'Let's play with Sammy,' he said, and he showed Nicola the soft snake he had retrieved, running his hands over the furry skin of it and petting it as if it was a real snake.

Nicola wasn't so sure about this toy as she didn't really like snakes, but she reluctantly petted it too, and Tony giggled when he saw her doing so. But then he froze when he heard the creak of a floorboard outside his bedroom, and his demeanour changed rapidly when he feared that somebody might be about to walk in on them.

'Get out!' he suddenly cried at Nicola, snatching the toy snake away and throwing it back under the bed before pointing at her and shouting again. 'Get out! Get out!'

Nicola had no idea why he was suddenly so panicked, not to mention aggressive, but he was making enough noise to give away the fact that she was in here now, so it was no surprise when the bedroom door opened and Barbara burst in, catching her in here with her son.

'I told her to get out, Mummy! I told her!' Tony cried, desperately trying to be believed, and while Nicola wasn't sure if his mum was buying it, she did notice how angry the woman looked.

'What are you doing in here?' she shouted at the girl on the carpet. 'I told you not to come in here!'

'I'm sorry! I just wanted to play!' Nicola tried, but it was no good because Barbara had already seized her by the arm and pulled her to her feet before marching her to the door, away from Tony and his toys.

'I'm going to have to tell your mother that you have been very naughty,' Barbara said as she hauled Nicola out into the hallway and closed the bedroom door behind her, denying the young girl the chance to see Tony one more time.

'No, please don't,' Nicola begged, afraid that she was going to get in a lot of trouble with her own parents. 'I'm sorry!'

Nicola didn't really know what she was sorry for, but she knew that apologising was usually the best thing to do in situations where she found herself in trouble with an adult, and she hoped it would work out for her again here. But Barbara was very angry, and she shook her head before grabbing Nicola's hand and marching her down the staircase and into the living room, where Bill was sitting in one of the armchairs.

Nicola had never been in this room before, and she looked around at the old television set and the large Grandfather clock before hearing Barbara tell her husband just what she had caught the girl doing upstairs. When she had finished, Bill picked up the remote control and turned the TV off before beckoning for Nicola to be brought closer to him, and when she was positioned in front of him, Nicola could feel his warm breath on her face. It was the same musty breath that she felt whenever they were alone together in the playroom, and the feeling of it made her just as frightened down here as it did up there.

‘Do you want to go back to the playroom?’ Bill asked her as he glared into her eyes, and Nicola shook her head firmly to answer that question. ‘Do you want to get in trouble with your parents?’ was the next question, and again, Nicola replied in the negative. ‘Do you want us to leave you alone?’ was the third question, and this time, Nicola had the chance to change her answer.

She nodded her head, and Bill seemed fine with that reply before leaning in even closer so that his face was right in front of hers, and she could feel his breath even more on her skin.

‘Good,’ he said. ‘We will leave you alone, and you won’t get in any trouble with your parents as long as you keep our secret. Got that?’

Nicola confirmed that she understood, and then Bill sat back in his chair and turned the TV on again, as calm and relaxed as if he hadn’t just been issuing a stern warning to a six-year-old girl. It was as if he had already forgotten about it, and by the time Ruth came to collect her daughter, Barbara acted as if she had forgotten about it too.

But Nicola could not forget. Despite never having to set foot in that house again after that day, she had never forgotten.

As the years had gone by, it seemed like that had been her punishment.

But perhaps one day, those memories could actually be of some service to her.

She just wouldn’t know how until the time came.

19

PRESENT DAY

'Please, just let me say goodbye to him,' Nicola begged the old woman who was still sitting beside the bed with Bill in. 'Just let me tell him that I love him. That's all I ask. Then you can do whatever you want to do, to him and to me.'

Nicola wasn't being quite truthful there because she was hoping that if her plan worked, no harm would come to either her or her nephew, but that remained to be seen. The first thing was convincing Barbara to allow Ben into this room to visit her with Tony by his side.

But would she go for it?

'Why should we do what you ask?' Barbara wanted to know, which seemed reasonable.

Fortunately, Nicola had a good answer for that one.

'Because I did what you asked of me,' she replied calmly. 'I kept our secret all these years. I didn't tell anybody what either of you did to me.'

Barbara thought about it for a moment before nodding her head. 'I suppose you did,' she said, showing almost a begrudging respect to her victim. 'You were certainly a lot better behaved than Ryan, that's for sure.'

'Then please, allow me this one last thing,' Nicola went on. 'You've already won. Just let me say goodbye to my nephew.'

Barbara seemed to like the younger woman's admission of defeat, and perhaps that was the tipping point in her deciding that Nicola could have what she wanted.

'It's a fair last request,' Barbara said as she rose to her feet and walked away from her husband in the bed. 'I will let you say goodbye to your nephew. But you will have to make it quick. My plan cannot accommodate any delays.'

Nicola nodded her head to show that she understood as she watched Barbara walk past her and reach the door. But before she could leave, the prisoner had one more thing to add.

'Can I say goodbye to Tony as well?' she asked, and that caused Barbara to pause.

'Why would you want to do that?'

'Because we're friends.'

Barbara scoffed at that notion, but Nicola did her best to try and stay convincing.

'I know it sounds silly, but I've always thought of us that way ever since we played together that time in his room,' she went on. 'And I know he is a good person. I would like to say goodbye to him too.'

Barbara thought about it before shrugging. 'He has to bring the boy in here anyway, so I suppose it won't do any harm,' she said before leaving the room and closing the door, and Nicola heard the sound of the key turning in the lock again.

Letting out a deep breath to relieve some of the tension that came from having just taken her one and only shot at getting out of here, Nicola could now only wait for that door to open and Ben and Tony to come in here. When they did, it would be time for the second part of her plan.

Nicola did her best not to spend too long looking at Bill in the bed as she waited for Barbara to return with her requested visitors, but she felt his eyes on her the entire time. It was a relief then when the key finally turned in the lock again, and the door opened, and it was certainly a sight for sore eyes when Nicola caught a glimpse of her little nephew standing in the doorway. He looked even smaller than usual, but that was only because he was standing beside Tony, and the man led him into the room as Barbara remained in the doorway behind them.

'Auntie Nicola!' Ben cried when he saw his family member tied up in the corner of the room, and he wanted to rush towards her, but Tony kept a grip on his shoulder, and that prevented him from getting any closer.

'I'm okay,' Nicola assured her nephew as best she could as she didn't want him to be any more afraid than he already was. 'What about you? Did they hurt you?'

Ben shook his head, so that was a relief to her, even though she knew that his suffering would begin in earnest if she was to fail with her plan and not make it out of this room before Barbara had her killed by whatever means the old woman had decided on.

'What about Mummy and Daddy?' Ben asked his auntie. 'And Grandma and Grandad? Are they okay?'

'Yes, they are okay too,' Nicola replied defiantly. 'They are just sleeping.'

‘I want to go and see them.’

‘I know. But first, you have to come here and give me a hug, okay?’

It was impossible for the prisoner to hold out her arms considering her wrists were still bound, but she hoped that Ben would be allowed to get closer to her because she had something very important that she wanted to say to him, and she needed to say it without anybody else hearing it.

‘Please, just one hug,’ Nicola said as she looked to Barbara to get the permission she needed for Tony to allow the little boy closer.

‘Quickly then,’ Barbara replied, letting out a sigh of frustration, and she told her son to allow Ben to go towards Nicola.

Tony let go of Ben’s shoulder, and the little boy rushed forward towards his auntie on the floor, and he wrapped his arms around her as he knelt beside her and hugged her tightly. It was difficult for Nicola to hold her emotion in at that moment because she could see and feel how frightened her nephew was, but she had to do it because this would be the only chance she got to speak to Ben privately.

‘I need you to listen to me,’ she whispered into his ear as he continued to hug her. ‘We’re going to play a game of hide and seek, okay?’

Ben suddenly pulled back slightly and looked at his auntie, but she asked him for one more hug, and he did as he was told, so that allowed her to speak to him again without being heard by anyone else in the room.

'When I shout the word run, I want you to run out of this room as fast as you can, and go and find a hiding place in this house, okay?'

Ben nodded his head.

'Promise me you will find a good hiding place, and don't come out unless I find you,' Nicola said, and Ben nodded again before Barbara called time on this goodbye.

'That's enough,' she said. 'Come on now, Ben. Time to go.'

Ben really didn't want to leave his auntie's side because he continued to hug her tightly, but she told him that everything was going to be okay, and he eventually let go of her and made his way back to Tony.

'Wait, you said I could say goodbye to Tony too,' Nicola cried, and Barbara paused before remembering that had been part of the deal.

'Quickly,' she said, and she told her son that Nicola wished to say bye to him as well.

Tony seemed very surprised by that, but he also looked excited, and Nicola smiled at him to let him know that she only had friendly intentions. As the man came towards her, he left Ben standing by himself in the middle of the room, and the young boy looked around, awkward and unsure about his surroundings, particularly when he noticed the old man in the bed. But Nicola remained focused on Tony, and as he reached her, she asked him to come down to her level.

The man crouched down beside her, and she smiled at him again before asking him if he remembered the time they had played together as children. Tony nodded his head, and Nicola said that it had been fun. Then she asked him if he wanted to play with her again, which Tony had to think about. He seemed unsure and looked back towards his mother in the doorway across the basement, but Nicola whispered that she would like to play more games but that he would need to untie her hands if they were going to be able to do that.

'What are you saying to him?' Barbara suddenly wanted to know, and she stepped into the room, creating more of a gap between her and the doorframe, and Nicola was pleased to see that because it would help Ben in a moment's time. But she had to focus on Tony for now, so she whispered to him again.

'Take this tape off my hands, and we can play together,' she said before gambling and saying the words she knew could make or break her whole plan. 'And maybe we can be boyfriend and girlfriend too.'

Tony seemed shocked by that suggestion, but Nicola smiled and nodded to prove to him that she had meant it.

'Would you like that?' she asked him, and this time, it was his turn to nod.

'Just take this tape off me, and we can be boyfriend and girlfriend then,' Nicola whispered, and she looked towards the man's pocket at where the scissors were still poking out.

'That's enough,' Barbara said as she stepped further into the room. 'Come on, Tony. Time to go.'

But Tony was torn about which woman to listen to. His mother or the girl next door.

'Please, Tony. I know you're a good person. Just cut this tape off me,' Nicola urged Tony again as Barbara got closer.

'Tony! Listen to me! I said it's time to go!' Barbara called.

But Tony ignored her, and then he reached for his pocket, removing the scissors and letting Nicola know that he wished to help her.

'What are you doing?' Barbara cried as she rushed towards him, but Tony had already made his mind up. He cut the tape around Nicola's wrists, and her hands were suddenly free.

'Ben, run!' she cried, and the young boy sprang into action just like his auntie had requested, sprinting towards the open door and making it through before Barbara could catch him.

In the chaos that her cry had caused, Nicola was able to grab the scissors from Tony's hand and use them to cut the tape around her legs before springing to her feet and running towards the door too.

Barbara turned around when she saw the woman coming towards her, and Nicola raised the scissors in her hand to show that she had a potentially deadly weapon that she wasn't afraid to use if she had to. But she wasn't expecting to need them because she presumed Barbara would back down in the face of violence.

Only she didn't.

She stood her ground and told Nicola she would never make it out of this house.

That was why Nicola acted.

She stuck the scissors into the side of the old woman's abdomen as she rushed past her, and she made it to the door, while Barbara howled in pain behind her.

As she ran for the door, Nicola's plan was to close it when she got through it and lock it behind her, trapping the family down in the basement and giving her own family a chance to end this nightmare before it got any worse. But the wounded Barbara instructed her son to give chase, and having seen what Nicola had just done to his mother, Tony set off after her with surprising speed and a dangerous determination.

Nicola ran through the door before pushing it closed, hoping that she could seal it before Tony reached it. She did, but just before she could turn the key that was in the lock, she felt herself almost get knocked off her feet.

It was the force of Tony's bodyweight on the other side of the door. He was trying to get through, and despite her best efforts, Nicola knew she wouldn't be able to keep him out forever.

She couldn't keep the door closed, no matter how hard she tried, and because of that, she knew she couldn't lock it and end the danger. Digging her shoulder into the surface of the door, Nicola cried out in pain as Tony pushed on the other side. But the door was opening further and further, and she knew she was losing the fight.

If the man got hold of her, then there was no saying what he might do to her after she had just stabbed his mother. Therefore, she had no other choice.

She gave up on trying to keep the door closed and just started running instead.

20

Sprinting up the basement steps, Nicola heard the sound of the door behind her swing open and hit the wall, a sure sign that Tony had made it through and was right on her tail. But she didn't look back to see how close he was to her. She just kept running, and after reaching the top of the steps, she saw that she had come out into the kitchen.

Trying the back door first, she found it locked, so she rushed into the hallway towards the front door, which she tried to pull open. But it was locked too, as she had feared but expected.

In her optimistic fantasy, she had envisioned one of the doors being open, and she could have run to a neighbour's house and begged for help, ensuring the police were swiftly called as Ben continued to stay hidden in his hiding place until help arrived on the scene. But things weren't going to be that simple, and she was going to have to find another way out of here.

The only problem was that she didn't have much time to look for one.

Tony's footsteps behind her forced her to spin around, and when she did, she saw the man standing in the hallway a few feet away from her.

'Why did you do that to my mummy?' he wanted to know.

'Because she is a bad person,' Nicola replied honestly. 'She tied me up, and she wanted to hurt Ben. You don't want her to do that, do you?'

'You hurt her.'

'I was defending myself. I was defending us.'

'I thought you liked me.'

'I do!'

'No, you don't. You wouldn't have hurt my mummy if you did.'

That was when Nicola realised that she was not going to be able to trick him into helping her this time. He was angry and upset, and most of all, he was stopping her from looking for another way out of here.

As he came towards her, Nicola tried to run into the living room, but Tony grabbed her before she could get there, and he pushed her back against the wall, holding her arms against it, so she was unable to fend him off.

'Please! Just let me go!' Nicola begged, pleading with the man who seemed to be her only way out of this. There was no saying how long it might take Barbara to recover from her injuries and make it up here, but Nicola knew that her task would only get more difficult when she did because Tony was unlikely to go against his mother's wishes then. Therefore, she had to convince him to let her go before that.

The problem was it didn't seem like he was letting her go.

If anything, he was starting to really hurt her.

Putting one of his hands around her throat, Nicola feared the worst, and she cried out for help before the pressure on her throat was too much for her to make any more sounds. She then resorted to trying to kick Tony, but he was still not letting go of her.

Was he really going to kill her?

The sound of a noise above their heads caused them both to look up the staircase behind them, and when they did, they saw Ben standing at the top of it. He had come out of his hiding place after hearing his auntie's cry for help, and when he saw her struggling, he begged Tony to let her go.

Tony's surprise at seeing the boy caused him to loosen his grip on Nicola's neck, and when he did, the woman seized her chance to get away from him, pushing him backwards before kicking him between the legs and running up the stairs towards Ben.

She grabbed him by the hand and looked around at the four doors up here while trying to figure out which one was the best one to go to, but with Tony back in pursuit, she didn't have time to be fussy.

Dragging Ben into Tony's bedroom, she instructed the boy to hide under the bed before she did her best to push a chest of drawers in front of the door to keep the room owner out. But she only got the drawers halfway across the door before Tony started pushing it back open, and once again, it was clear he was going to overpower her and get through to her.

Giving up on the losing battle, Nicola backed away and stood in front of the bed, putting her hands out in front of herself and pleading with Tony not to come any closer.

'Please! Just let us go! You don't need to hurt us, and none of this is your fault! You won't get in any trouble!' Nicola cried, hoping that could convince the man to open the front door and allow them to leave. 'We can still be friends, and we can still play together like we did before, okay?'

Reaching out for a figurine of a soldier that was on Tony's bedside table, she held it out towards the man to show him that she would be happy to play if he was, and that seemed to change his state of mind.

'You want to play?' he asked Nicola as he looked at the figurine, and while she hadn't been meaning to do it now, she didn't want to disappoint him now that he had seemingly been placated.

'Okay! Sure! Let's play now,' Nicola said. 'What do you want to play?'

As Tony looked around the room for a game, Nicola looked down at the bed beside her where she knew Ben was hiding underneath. As long as he stayed quiet then he would be safe, and she would have more time to find a way out of here.

'Let's play with this,' Tony said, and he picked up a plastic sword from the top of the dresser table that Nicola had unsuccessfully tried to drag in front of the door.

He handed the sword to her before picking up a second one, presumably so they could have a friendly duel, but before that happened, Nicola needed to tell him some things.

'I need to go to my house and see my family,' she told him. 'I need to check if they're okay.'

'Fight first,' Tony replied, and he hit his sword against Nicola's, causing a loud sound as the two pieces of plastic collided.

'If you let me and Ben go next door to see our family, then I promise we can play then,' Nicola tried as Tony got more into the game.

'You're not very good at this,' he said as he continued to strike her sword before playfully tapping her on the arm with his 'weapon.'

'If I win, can we go next door to see my family?' she asked him, and Tony thought about it for a moment before agreeing.

'But you won't win!' he said with a laugh before he began jumping around the room and striking her sword.

Nicola tried to keep up with him, but this was hardly her game, and this was hardly working. She needed to get out of here and fast, not just to check on her family but also to give Barbara less time to get out of that basement and get Tony back on side.

'Please, Tony, let us go,' Nicola said as she half-heartedly jabbed at him, but Tony was playing a lot harder than her, and he clearly was in no mood to let her win or leave this room. He was having too much fun.

'Tony! Please! Let us leave!' Nicola cried when she became exasperated with the childish man in front of her. But her raised voice snapped him out of his silly game, and he lowered his sword as he looked at his neighbour.

'This isn't fun,' he said as he put his sword down. 'I want to do something else.'

'Like what?'

'I want to kiss.'

Nicola stepped backwards as Tony approached her, and she stumbled as her legs hit the bedframe, and she lost her balance, sitting down on the duvet and trying to get back up before he could reach her.

'Do you still want to be my girlfriend?' Tony asked as he sat beside her.

'I don't know,' she told him. 'That depends if you will let me go home.'

'If we are boyfriend and girlfriend, then we need to kiss.'

He closed his eyes and puckered his lips but didn't move his face any closer towards hers, and Nicola wanted to run for the door again, but she knew it was pointless. Not only would she be leaving Ben behind under this bed, but she knew by now that she couldn't outrun Tony, and the only doors out of this house were locked.

But what else could she do?

Tony opened his eyes and looked at her as if to ask why she hadn't kissed him when he had been ready.

'What are you doing?' he wanted to know.

'I don't feel well,' Nicola tried, but Tony didn't seem to care.

'Kiss me,' he said again, and this time he put his hand behind her head and moved her skull towards his.

He closed his eyes again and puckered his lips, but Nicola tried to force her head away from him, although he didn't like that.

'Kiss me!' he repeated, but the undertones of aggression were more obvious now, and as he moved himself on top of her, trapping her underneath him, she began to panic.

'Stop it!' she tried, but he wouldn't get off her, forcing her body deeper into the mattress as he started to kiss her himself, moving his lips across hers in a very awkward manner. But he seemed to be enjoying it, and he didn't even stop when Ben crawled out from underneath the bed and started trying to pull him off his auntie.

Nicola's arms and legs thrashed around as she tried to get out from underneath the heavy man, but it wasn't working. Neither were Ben's continued attempts. It was obvious that she needed something to hit Tony with, and she hung her arm over the edge of the bed and reached around for anything she might be able to grab a hold of and use as a weapon.

Her fingers found something furry beneath the bed, and she pulled it up to see that it was a toy she recognised. It was Sammy The Snake, and she began to hit Tony with the body of it, hoping that would be enough to get him to stop. But it wasn't causing him any pain, thanks to how soft it was, and Nicola was just about to let go of it and try and find something else when she had an idea.

Wrapping the snake around Tony's neck, she tightened it as hard as she could, suffocating the man and making it impossible for him not to respond this time.

Tony lifted his head up immediately and tried to pull the snake off from where it was squeezing his neck, but Nicola refused to loosen her grip on it, and she kept strangling him, the rage inside her now being fully unleashed after this day from hell.

As Tony gasped for air, Nicola refused to let up, and she kept the snake around his neck even as he rolled off her and onto the bed next to her. She kept pulling as he kicked his legs and slapped his hands against her, and she only stopped when Tony stopped moving.

She didn't even check if he was dead or just unconscious after that.

She just grabbed Ben's hand and ran from the room.

Running back downstairs, Nicola led Ben into the living room, but she was not going to waste any time now trying to open locked doors. Instead, she just picked up the small coffee table and threw it against the window, shattering the pane of glass and finally giving the pair an escape route.

'Be careful,' she told her nephew as she lifted him up so that he could get through the broken window, and Nicola joined him once he was safely outside. Then she held his hand tightly as they slipped and skidded their way through the thick snow in order to get back to the house next door and check on the state of the people inside.

When they entered the home, Nicola told Ben to wait in the hallway before she went in search of her other family members, worried that they might not be in a good way, and she was protecting the young boy from seeing anything that might have scarred him for life. But when she located her family, she found them upstairs, her parents lying on their bed, while Colin and Charlotte were on the bed in the spare room. Checking their pulses, she found that they were just unconscious, and it was obvious they would have laid here while the fire had engulfed this home if only Nicola hadn't been able to thwart her neighbours' deadly plan.

But now that she had, there was only one thing left to do. She called the emergency services and told them what had happened. Then she waited, and she prayed.

She prayed for the best for her family members.

And she prayed for the worst for the family next door.

21

Nicola knew that it would be nigh on impossible to have another family meal quite as dramatic as the last time she had sat around a table with her relatives, and she was pleased that this particular occasion was passing by without incident. Not only was this the first time they had all sat together at dinner since the crazy events of Christmas Day, but this would also be the last time she would see her relatives for a while. Nicola's flight back to Australia was due to depart England tomorrow morning, and when she boarded that plane, she knew she wouldn't be back on these shores for several months. It was time to go back to the life she had made for herself Down Under, not because she was running away from anything anymore, but because she had unfinished business there. But first, it was all about enjoying these last few hours with the people she had fought so hard to save.

'Is everything okay with your meal?' the pleasant waiter in the smart white shirt asked the diners who were all hungrily tucking into their food, and only those who didn't have a mouthful of whatever they had ordered at that exact moment in time were able to answer him in the affirmative.

Nicola was one of those who had been too busy scoffing to give a reply, but she did offer a thumbs up to the waiter before he walked away and went to check on the next table in this busy Italian restaurant. Then she returned to consuming her bowl of Spaghetti Carbonara, wolfing down the tasty meal as she continued her recovery from the ordeal she had been through down in her neighbours' basement.

Having managed to not only escape from Bill, Barbara, and Tony, but get the medical assistance that her family required in order to ensure they were able to survive too, no one could argue that she didn't deserve to be eating well today. Despite those dark moments down in the basement when it seemed like her world was ending and that everyone she had ever held dear was going to suffer at the hands of her despicable neighbours just like she herself had done in the past, her worst fears had not come true.

Everybody had survived.

At least everybody in her family anyway.

But the same could not be said for the family next door. There had been a death there, not that Nicola was too concerned about it. The deceased had been seventy-three, and she had bled to death on the floor of the basement in front of her husband, who was supposed to have died months earlier.

Barbara was no more, the stab wound to her abdomen proving fateful after the scissors that Nicola stabbed into her had punctured an artery that had caused her to bleed out in what most likely would have only been a few minutes. That explained why Barbara had not emerged from the basement to pursue Nicola and Ben, and it also explained why the killer had been made to spend so much time talking to the police in the aftermath.

It would be safe to say that the scene that awaited the police officers and paramedics when they had arrived at both houses in the early hours of Boxing Day had been a confronting one. With most of Nicola's family still drugged from the poisoned lemon cake in their house, while Barbara had bled to death and Tony lay unconscious on an upstairs bed with a toy snake wrapped around his neck next door, the emergency services had certainly had their work cut out deciphering it all. But it was, perhaps, the sight of the old man in the bed in the basement that had given them the biggest surprise, because it didn't take the police long to figure out that this was a man who had supposedly passed away already, sparing him from a court case that could have seen him convicted on various sex offences.

With the old man taken into custody while the memory of his wife dying right in front of his eyes played out in his mind over and over again, it had been no surprise to learn that Bill was not doing so well in the hospital prison wing he was currently being kept in. But that was not Nicola's concern. What had been her concern was making sure that she got her story straight with the police officers who had interviewed her for several long hours as they had tried to piece together exactly what had occurred in both houses during that very dramatic Christmas that would never be forgotten by those who were a part of it.

Nicola had experienced no trouble in telling the tale of how Barbara had poisoned her family and how the old woman had kept her locked in the basement, as well as the evil plan she had concocted that involved her young nephew. Nor had she struggled to recount what Barbara had told her about why Bill had faked his own death and had been living a secret life in that same basement. But where she had struggled was when she had needed to clarify things that had happened long before that fateful Christmas Day. The police had wanted to know about Nicola's history with the family next door, and while she felt like she could have gotten away with keeping the past abuse to herself, she forced herself to confront her demons and let the officers know exactly how vile her parents' neighbours had been towards her and others.

Having initially worried that speaking about the abuse she had suffered in the past might have given the police a possible motive to charge her for the murder of Barbara and the attempted murder of Tony, she had not had to worry about that once she had finished speaking. Not only were the police satisfied that she had simply acted in whatever way she needed to to try and survive the ordeal and save her family, but they were hardly in a rush to punish her for what she had done in retaliation to the horrors she had faced both recently and in the past. They had let her leave the police station a short time after she had finished giving her statement and answering all the questions, and as she had made her way out into the car park, Nicola felt as if a weight had been lifted from her shoulders.

For the first time in her life, she had told another person about what had happened to her in her childhood.

The police knew.

Then it was time for her family to know.

If it had been difficult for her to bear her soul in the interview room, then it had been even harder when she had sat in front of her parents and brother that evening and told them what she had told the police. She told John, Ruth, and Colin all about the abuse she had suffered at the hands of Bill and how Barbara had not only allowed it to happen, but had engineered it to be as easy as possible for her husband to partake in.

Her mother had wept as she had heard the sorry tale of what had really happened when she had left her daughter in the seemingly capable hands of the next-door neighbours, while John had just stared solemnly down at the carpet, almost unable to look his daughter in the eye, not out of shame, but out of anger and sheer shock. And then there had been Colin, the brother who, having learnt what his poor sister had been through, could only have felt guilty about his swimming races being the reason why she was left next door by herself in the first place. But having finished telling the sad story, Nicola had made it clear that none of what had happened was her family's fault, nor did she blame any of them for how things had transpired.

They were not to know. They had done nothing wrong.

And it was over now, in more ways than one.

The four of them had hugged and wept after that, their sobs muffled as they had buried their tear-stained faces in each other's shoulders and tried to make some sense of it all. But by the time they had separated and looked each other in the eyes, there had been a new, deeper level to their love for each other. Nicola had felt it, and she was certain that her other family members had felt it too. Despite the horrors of what had happened, they were still strong, and most importantly, they had survived. If Nicola felt okay enough to move forward with her life, then they could do the same thing, and that was what they were trying to do now as they dined in this restaurant and tried to be as normal a family as possible.

John's anger was still bubbling away beneath the surface, but that had been tempered somewhat by both Barbara's death and the fact that Bill was now in police custody and would never be a free man again. Ruth's horror at what her poor daughter had been subjected to as a child would never really diminish, but she was working hard to focus on the positive parts of Nicola's childhood, of which Nicola assured her mum there had been many. And Colin was doing his best to play his usual role of the annoying older brother still, teasing Nicola over the size of her meal and her choice of dress for today's occasion because he knew that was how his sister not only expected him to be, but wanted him to be.

She was moving on, and so too must they.

As for little Ben, he had recovered from it all the quickest, and having finished his pizza in record-breaking time, he was now playing with a little plastic car while Charlotte sat beside him and kept an eye on him so that he didn't make too much noise to disturb the other diners.

Overall, that last night Nicola spent with her family in England was a very happy occasion, and by the time she boarded her plane the following morning, she had a big smile on her face. She was going back to Australia, and she was sad to say goodbye to her relatives again, but she felt closer to them all than ever before.

Being back on the other side of the world to each other would not come between them.

Certainly not if Bill and Barbara's actions had failed to do so from the house right next door.

If she had one regret as she departed the UK, it was that she hadn't had a chance to speak with any of Bill and Barbara's other victims, although she had left her phone number with one of the support staff who were tasked with getting statements from as many victims as she could. She wondered if anybody would call and want to talk to her. Perhaps Eric Morgan would, the boy who had grown up a few houses down on Nicola's street, and the person who Barbara had referenced back in that playroom many years ago as having partaken in the twisted games Bill liked to play. She had always wanted to speak with him over the years about their shared ordeal, but it had seemed too hard.

Maybe one day.

Then there was Ryan, the boy who had been the first victim brave enough to alert the police, only to see Bill get off the hook for his crimes by faking his death. Ryan was still very young, and maybe his time for processing what he had been through would come much later. Either way, Nicola would be happy to speak with him too if it could help either of them process their pain.

But for now, Nicola was on her own again, although she didn't plan to keep it that way for much longer.

She had big plans for when she got back to Australia.

Plans that would prove she really had put Bill and Barbara behind her.

22

After spending Christmas in the freezing cold Northern hemisphere, Nicola felt rejuvenated now that she was back basking in the heat that was summertime in Sydney. It was hard for her to believe that she had been trudging through thick snow on her parents' driveway only a couple of days before, yet here she was now, standing on the warm sands of Bondi beach wearing nothing more than a teeny bikini and attracting the admiring glances of several of the men who she was sharing this desirable sunbathing spot with. But Nicola did not have eyes for any of those men. She only had eyes for the man who was sitting right beside her now in his black shorts. It was Harrison, the dishy doctor whom she had initially begun dating a year ago, only for that short-lived romance to end in a very awkward fashion.

Amazingly, despite Nicola having pushed this man into the harbour after becoming uncomfortable with the intimacy of their first kiss, the doctor had been surprisingly receptive to her text message yesterday asking him if he wanted to meet up again, and this time his swimming attire made him better prepared were he to get wet again. But now Nicola and Harrison had been reunited, the Englishwoman was determined to have this date go better than their last one had.

She wanted them to kiss again, only this time, she was desperate not to let the pain of her past get in the way of the happiness of her future.

‘So, how does it feel to be back?’ Harrison asked Nicola as they sat on the towels they had laid on the hot sand and stared out at all the swimmers splashing around in the waves. ‘Missing the English winter?’

‘I wouldn’t say I’m missing it,’ Nicola said with a smile as she reached into her bag for the bottle of Factor 30 that she knew she had in there for occasions like this. ‘I don’t think there are too many people in my hometown who are putting sun cream on right now.’

Harrison laughed as he watched Nicola apply some of the cream to her arms before she offered him the bottle. He gratefully accepted it, apologising for forgetting to bring his own before rubbing some cream into his neck and preventing it from getting any redder than it had already become.

‘When are you due back at work?’ he asked her a moment later, once the bottle was back in the bag and the tanning could recommence without the fear of sunburn ruining the fun.

‘The day after tomorrow.’

‘Wow, one more day of leave? You really are making the most of Christmas.’

‘Yeah, I better had. I’m going to be working for the next several months before my next holiday.’

Nicola rolled her eyes, trying to make light of the fact that her annual leave count was now very depleted and would take a long time to be replenished again. But she knew that she had done well to even get time off over Christmas and be able to spend the holiday with her family because many of her colleagues had seen their leave denied and had been forced to work long shifts instead of opening presents and tucking into turkeys. Therefore, she couldn't really grumble too much about the fact that it wouldn't be long until she was back on a hospital ward, rushed off her feet and feeling a million miles away from this carefree atmosphere on the beach.

'So, what did you get up to back in England?' Harrison wanted to know as he ran his fingers through the hot sand and disturbed the grains in a playful manner. 'Besides eating lots of homecooked food and having snowball fights?'

Nicola knew that answering that question honestly would most likely cause the doctor beside her to grab his towel and run away down the beach as fast as his legs could carry him, so she decided not to be too truthful, at least not yet anyway. If things went well between them today and in the near future, then she would feel more comfortable about sharing her experiences with him, those of the Christmas just gone as well as those in her distant past. But right now, it was not the time or the place to get heavy and spoil the great mood they were both in. That was why she just told him that she had spent her time back in England catching up with old friends, drinking and eating too much, and relaxing with her family.

She told him what Santa had brought her nephew, she relayed a few of the teasing taunts she had endured from her brother, and she recounted the stories of her parents and how happy they had been to have their daughter home again for a short while.

'It sounds very wholesome,' Harrison said with a smile. 'A proper British Christmas.'

'Yeah, I guess it was,' Nicola replied, choosing to focus on the good rather than the bad and visualising her relatives' smiling faces in the times that had been less stressful.

'What about you?' Nicola wanted to know. 'Did you miss me around the hospital?'

'Of course. You know me, I always spend my shifts on the lookout for the nurse who pushed me in the harbour last year, so it was disappointing to see that you weren't around.'

Nicola laughed again after being reminded of that very awkward night the last time she had been with Harrison outside of a work setting. But today was a new day, and feeling a strong sense of purpose to show herself and others how much she had changed after everything she had been through, Nicola decided that there was no time like the present to do just that.

'You know, I was thinking about that night while I was on the plane back,' she confessed to Harrison as he continued to run his fingers through the sand. 'I was thinking about how I wished I had handled the kiss differently.'

'I wish you had handled it differently too,' Harrison admitted jokingly, and they shared a smile before Nicola continued with her train of thought.

'How about we try again?' she suggested, looking from his eyes to his lips and hoping that he got the strong hint.

'I would very much like that,' Harrison replied, and he stopped playing with the sand to give this moment the full attention that it deserved.

While Nicola imagined the man beside her was a little nervous about this moment right here, it surely paled in comparison to how she was feeling about it. But she was not going to be denied happiness any longer when it came to intimacy and relationships. She wanted to put the pain of her past behind her, and this here today, coupled with the counselling sessions that she had committed to attending with a therapist who specialised in child abuse cases, meant that she wasn't going to panic and push Harrison into any water now.

As their lips met, Nicola's heart was hammering in her chest, and she almost felt herself sinking deeper into the sand as if the heat of the moment was melting her, along with the heat from the searing sun overhead.

But she wasn't melting, at least not physically anyway.

She was just enjoying the kiss.

After their second kiss had gone a lot better than their first, Nicola and Harrison were able to enjoy a very relaxing afternoon in each other's company, splitting their time between sunbathing and snogging on the sand, and splashing around in the sea while trying not to think too much about the fact that there could be sharks out there somewhere that were just as hungry as any human being was around the Christmas dinner table.

By the time the sun was setting over Sydney and the sunseekers had headed inside to spend a warm night relaxing at home, Nicola and Harrison were holding hands and excitedly planning future dates together. But that wasn't all the woman was excited about. She was excited to let her family know that she was officially dating someone now. They would surely be happy about that and not just because of all that she had been through. It was because it would give them all yet another reason to want to board a plane and fly out to visit her in the new year, and she could not be unhappy about that.

After a very eventful Christmas, full of plenty of bad but also lots of good, Nicola felt positive.

She felt like she had won.

And she felt like she was now proving it to herself, to her loved ones, and to that evil old man who was in a prison hospital somewhere back in frigid England, alone and handcuffed to his bed while still mourning the loss of his despicable wife.

EPILOGUE

While the fireworks exploded high above the snow-covered town and the first few strains of 'Auld Lang Syne' began to be spouted in pubs, clubs, and houses all over this part of the world, there was one place that was decidedly devoid of all cheer and goodwill. That place was the prison where the town's criminals were kept under lock and key, and it was a place where the latest prisoner to be put into custody was lying, staring up at the flashing lights through the window and listening to the happy voices of all those hearty souls who were welcoming in a new year.

This private room in the hospital ward in the west wing of this prison was hardly the best place to spend such a momentous time on the calendar, but for Bill Wainwright, this was the place where he would see in what was most likely to be the last year of his life. Considering his age and his ill health, not to mention the environment he was now forced to reside in, it didn't seem likely that he would still be alive in twelve months to add another digit to the gravestone he would eventually be buried beneath.

The gravestone that would actually be real this time.

There weren't many people who got to live twice, but Bill was one of those people, having successfully faked his own death, at least for a while anyway. Now his secret was out, and he was paying for his crimes, all of them and in varying degrees of sentencing that would be decided on at a later date, but for now, he was consoling himself with the fact that he had led a long life and a remarkable one at that. That life of his had been shared for the most part with his wife, Barbara, and it was the fact that she had departed this Earth and left him behind for real that was the most difficult thing to bear as he continued to listen to, or be tortured by, the sounds of the free members of society celebrating the arrival of January 1st.

Barbara had recently passed away on the floor of the basement beneath their home, stabbed by Nicola, the neighbour who the couple had babysat for on several occasions. But the fact that Nicola was still free after what she had done was a testament to the crimes that the old couple had committed against her, and as he lay on his sickbed, one skeletal wrist shackled by a handcuff that was fastened to the bedrail beside him, Bill thought about what he had done with his life.

The sins he had committed. The pain he had caused. And the lives he had destroyed.

Was he full of remorse or regret? No, he was too old for anything like that. In his current state, he was as grateful for still breathing as he was frustrated at the fact that his youth was a distant memory and one he could never relive no matter how much he might wish for it. If anything, the old man just felt sad. He was sad because he had lost his wife, but he was also sad because their plan hadn't worked. They hadn't been able to keep Ben imprisoned, the young boy from next door having escaped thanks to the help of his auntie, who had also been able to save her family from the grim fate that had been planned for them. That meant he wasn't able to satisfy some of the urges that he still had, urges that had seen his life forever intertwined with far more innocent souls who had not deserved to ever have to cross paths with a person like him.

But as the fireworks fizzled out and the singing stopped, Bill afforded himself a wry smile. It was the smile of a man who felt he wasn't done yet.

There was life in the old dog, as they say.

Or at least there was until someone put a pillow over the old man's head and stopped him from being able to breathe.

But that person didn't care as he watched Bill die. He didn't care because he knew he was doing the right thing. He was killing a person who deserved to die.

Most of all, he was killing the person who had caused him so much pain.

The janitor removed the pillow when he was done, and after double-checking to make sure that evil old man was really dead, he walked out of the room, taking his mop and bucket with him.

Passing the prison officer who was sitting on guard outside the room, the janitor wondered if he was going to be called back at a later date when the deceased was discovered. But he hoped not, and he almost didn't expect to be. After all, an ill and very elderly sex offender had just died in hospital. There didn't seem to be much mystery there, nor did it seem like any police officer would be breaking their necks to look into the loss of the life of such a despised figure.

Returning to the cleaner's closet, the janitor put away his tools of the trade before taking a deep breath and thinking about who he had just done that for. He had done it for himself, mostly, but he had also done it for his neighbour, Nicola, whose story had just been in the local news and for anybody else whose life had been ruined by that evil man. Then he decided to carry on with his duties, looking forward to the next time he would visit his parents' home on that street where Bill and Barbara used to live. Their house was for sale now, and pretty soon it would be sold, allowing a new family to move in and make some better memories in that home.

The janitor couldn't wait for that to happen, and to prove how happy he was now, he whistled a tune as he made his way out of the cupboard and down the corridor of the hospital prison wing where he had worked for the last six years. He whistled a Christmas song, and he whistled it loud and proud.

The festive period might have just passed, but Eric Morgan had just given himself a belated present.

Merry Christmas indeed.

Download My Free Book

If you would like to receive a FREE copy of my psychological thriller 'Just One Second', then you can find the link to the book at my website www.danielhurstbooks.com

Thank you for reading *No Time To Be Alone*. If you have enjoyed this psychological thriller, then you'll be pleased to know that I have several more stories in this genre, and you can find a list of my titles on the next page, including my bestselling book *Til Death Do Us Part*, which has a twist that very few people have been able to predict so far…

ALSO BY DANIEL HURST

TIL DEATH DO US PART
THE PASSENGER
THE WOMAN AT THE DOOR
HE WAS A LIAR
THE BROKEN VOWS
THE WRONG WOMAN
THE TUTOR
THE NEIGHBOURS
RUN AWAY WITH ME
THE ROLE MODEL
THE BOYFRIEND
THE PROMOTION

(All books available now on Amazon and on Kindle Unlimited – read on to learn a little more about them...)

TIL DEATH DO US PART

What if your husband was your worst enemy?

Megan thinks that she has the perfect husband and the perfect life. Craig works all day so that she doesn't have to, leaving her free to relax in their beautiful and secluded country home. But when she starts to long for friends and purpose again, Megan applies for a job in London, much to her husband's disappointment. She thinks he is upset because she is unhappy. But she has no idea.

When Megan secretly attends an interview and meets a recruiter for a drink, Craig decides it is time to act. Locking her away in their home, Megan realises that her husband never had her best interests at heart. Worse, they didn't meet by accident. Craig has been planning it all from the start.

As Megan is kept shut away from the world with only somebody else's diary for company, she starts to uncover the lies, the secrets, and the fact that she isn't actually Craig's first wife after all...

THE PASSENGER

She takes the same train every day. But this is a journey she will never forget...

Amanda is a hardworking single mum, focused on her job and her daughter, Louise. But it's also time she did something for herself, and after saving for years, she is now close to quitting her dreary 9-5 and following her dream.

But then, on her usual commute home from London to Brighton, she meets a charming stranger – a man who seems to know everything about her. Then he delivers an ultimatum. She needs to give him the code to her safe where she keeps her savings before they reach Brighton – or she will never see Louise again.

Amanda is horrified, but while she knows the threat is real, she can't give him the code. That's because the safe contains something other than her money. It holds a secret. *A secret so terrible it will destroy both her's and her daughter's life if it ever gets out...*

THE WRONG WOMAN

What if you were the perfect person to get revenge?

Simone used to be the woman other women would use if they suspected their partner was cheating. She would investigate, find out the truth and if the men were guilty, exact revenge in one form or another. But after things went wrong with one particular couple, Simone was forced to go into hiding to evade the law.

Having assumed a new identity, Simone is now Mary, a mild-mannered woman who doesn't raise her voice or get angry, meaning nobody would ever suspect her of being capable of the things she used to do for a living. But when she finds out that her new boyfriend is having an affair, it awakens in her the person she used to be. Plotting revenge, Mary reverts back to the woman she once was before she went on the run and became domesticated. That means Simone is back, and it also means that her boyfriend and his mistress are in for the shock of their lives.

They messed with her. *But they picked the wrong woman.*

THE WOMAN AT THE DOOR

It was a perfect Saturday night. ***Until she knocked on the door...***

Rebecca and Sam are happily married and enjoying a typical Saturday night until a knock at the door changes everything. There's a woman outside, and she has something to say. Something that will change the happy couple's relationship forever...

With their marriage thrown into turmoil, Rebecca no longer knows who to trust, while Sam is determined to find out who that woman was and why she came to their house. But the problem is that he doesn't know who she is and why she has targeted them.

Desperate to save his marriage, Sam is willing to do anything to find the truth, even if it means breaking the law. But as time goes by and things only seem to get worse, it looks like he could lose Rebecca forever.

THE NEIGHBOURS

It seemed like the perfect house on the perfect street. ***Until they met the neighbours...***

Happily married couple, Katie and Sean, have plenty to look forward to as they move into their new home and plan for the future. But then they meet two of their new neighbours, and everything on their quiet street suddenly doesn't seem as desirable as it did before.

Having been warned about the other neighbours and their adulterous and criminal ways, Katie and Sean realise that they are going to have to be on their guard if they want to make their time here a happy one.

But some of the other neighbours seem so nice, and that's why they choose to ignore the warning and get friendly with the rest of the people on the street. *And that is why their marriage will never be the same again...*

THE TUTOR

What if you invited danger into your home?

Amy is a loving wife and mother to her husband, Nick, and her two children, Michael and Bella. It's that dedication to her family that causes her to seek help for her teenage son when it becomes apparent that he is going to fail his end of school exams.

Enlisting the help of a professional tutor, Amy is certain that she is doing the best thing for her son and, indeed, her family. But when she discovers that there is more to this tutor than meets the eye, it is already too late.

With the rest of her family enamoured by the tutor, Amy is the only one who can see that there is something not quite right about her. But as the tutor becomes more involved in Amy's family, it's not just the present that is threatened. Secrets from the past are exposed too, and by the time everything is out in the open, Amy isn't just worried about her son and his exams anymore. She is worried for the survival of her entire family.

HE WAS A LIAR

What if you never really knew the man you loved?

Sarah is in a loving relationship with Paul, a seemingly perfect man who she is hoping to marry and start a family with one day, until his sudden death sends her into a world of pain.

Trying to come to terms with her loss, Sarah finds comfort in going through some of Paul's old things, including his laptop and his emails. But after finding something troubling, Sarah begins to learn things about Paul that she never knew before, and it turns out he wasn't as perfect as she thought. But as she unravels more about his secretive past, she ends up not only learning things that break her heart, but things that the police will be interested to know too.

Sarah can't believe what she has discovered. But it's only when she keeps digging that she realises it's not just her late boyfriend's secrets that are contained on the laptop. Other people's secrets are too, and they aren't dead, which means they will do anything to protect them.

RUN AWAY WITH ME

What if your partner was wanted by the police?

Laura is feeling content with her life. She is married, she has a good home, and she is due to give birth to her first child any day now. But her perfect world is shattered when her husband comes home flustered and afraid. He's made a terrible mistake. He's done a bad thing. *And now the police are going to be looking for him.*

There's only one way out of this. He wants to run. *But he won't go without his wife...*

Laura knows it is wrong. She knows they should stay and face the music. But she doesn't want to lose her man. She can't raise this baby alone. *So she agrees to go with him.* But life on the run is stressful and unpredictable, and as time goes by, Laura worries she has made a terrible mistake. They should never have ran. But it's too late for that now. Her life is ruined. The only question is: *how will it end?*

THE ROLE MODEL

She raised her. Now she must help her…

Heather is a single mum who has always done what's best for her daughter, Chloe. From childhood up to the age of seventeen, Chloe has been no trouble. That is until one night when she calls her mother with some shocking news. There's been an accident. *And now there's a dead body…*

As always, Heather puts her daughter's safety before all else, but this might be one time when she goes too far. Instead of calling the emergency services, Heather hides the body, saving her daughter from police interviews and public outcry.

But as she well knows, everything she does has an impact on her child's behaviour, and as time goes on and the pair struggle to keep their sordid secret hidden, Heather begins to think that she hasn't been such a good mum after all. *In fact, she might have been the worst role model ever…*

THE BROKEN VOWS

He broke his word to her. Now she wants revenge…

Alison is happily married to Graham, or at least she is until she finds out that he has been cheating on her. Graham has broken the vows he made on his wedding day. How could he do it? It takes Alison a while to figure it out, but at least she has time on her side. *Only that is where she is wrong.*

A devastating diagnosis means the clock is ticking down on her life now, and if she wants revenge on her cheating partner, then she is going to have to act fast. Alison does just that, implementing a dangerous and deadly plan, and it's one that will have far reaching consequences for several people, including her clueless husband.

INFLUENCE

Would you kill for a million followers?

Emily Bennett dreams of being a social media influencer, just like her idols, Mason Manor & Ivy Lane. But shortly after Ivy's untimely death, she is contacted by a secretive businessman who offers her the chance at the fame and fortune she so desperately craves.

While Emily initially gets to experience the things she has always wanted, it soon becomes clear that her new employer had sinister motives for approaching her, and it isn't long before she discovers that the life of her dreams comes with the kind of conditions that are the stuff of nightmares.

Social media isn't life or death.

It's more important than that.

THE 20 MINUTE SERIES

20 Chapters. 20 Characters. 20 intertwining stories.

An original psychological thriller series showing how we are all more connected to each other than we think.

What readers are saying:

"If you like people watching then you will love these books!"

"The psychological insight was fascinating, the stories were absorbing and the characters were 3D. I absolutely loved it."

"The books in this series are an incredibly easy read, you become invested in the lives of the characters so easily and I am eager to know more and more. Roll on the next book."

THE 20 MINUTES SERIES (in order)

20 MINUTES ON THE TUBE
20 MINUTES LATER
20 MINUTES IN THE PARK
20 MINUTES ON HOLIDAY
20 MINUTES BY THE THAMES
20 MINUTES AT HALLOWEEN
20 MINUTES AROUND THE BONFIRE
20 MINUTES BEFORE CHRISTMAS
20 MINUTES OF VALENTINE'S DAY
20 MINUTES TO CHANGE A LIFE
20 MINUTES IN LAS VEGAS
20 MINUTES IN THE DESERT
20 MINUTES ON THE ROAD
20 MINUTES BEFORE THE WEDDING
20 MINUTES IN COURT
20 MINUTES BEHIND BARS

About The Author

Daniel Hurst lives in the North West of England with his wife, Harriet, and considers himself extremely fortunate to be able to write stories every day for his readers.

You can visit him at his online home www.danielhurstbooks.com

You can connect with Daniel on Facebook at www.facebook.com/danielhurstbooks or on Instagram at www.instagram.com/danielhurstbooks

He is always happy to receive emails from readers at daniel@danielhurstbooks.com and replies to every single one.

Thank you for reading.

Daniel

Printed in Great Britain
by Amazon

74075851R00156